ASTEROIDEA

ASTEROIDEA

A novel

by

STEPHANIE A. SMITH

Adelaide Books

New York / Lisbon

2020

ASTEROIDEA
A novel
By Stephanie A. Smith

Published by Adelaide Books, New York / Lisbon
adelaidebooks.org

Editor-in-Chief
Stevan V. Nikolic

For any information, please address Adelaide Books
at info@adelaidebooks.org

or write to:

Adelaide Books
244 Fifth Ave. Suite D27
New York, NY, 10001

ISBN: 978-1-953510-76-1

Printed in the United States of America

This novel is dedicated to the late Toni Morrison, who endured an entire semester of me asking questions and talking with her during her office hours at UC Berkeley in the late 1980's. Her grace, her patience, her wisdom and above all her words kept the wind in my sails during the stormiest of years.

Contents

Acknowledgements

The author would like to thank both Nella Larsen and Sylvia Plath for inspiration; and her mentors Ursula K. Le Guin and Michael Cunningham for their long-term support, encouragement, and above all for their incisive minds; I would also like to acknowledge and thank the Noepe Center for the Literary Arts, for the writer's residency that allowed me to finish this manuscript, and to the University of Florida's Rothman Fellowship, for providing financial support. Finally, I would thank my mother Carol Marie and my sister Jennifer Carol, for everything.

Chapter One

A Splash Quite Unnoticed

Fear and love woke Claire Holt. Her eyelids snapped up, her pulse beat to a rumba all because she was about to catch a Sunday morning flight, post 9/11. The mere idea of flight is *impossible*, she thought, rubbing her face roughly. *I can't…* then she shook herself. She would, even though parting from her youngest daughter, Ruth, had become so difficult of late that she got the shakes. *Ruthie's all grown up*, she chided herself, but no amount of common sense could quiet the jumping bean of her heart. Letting go of her elder daughter had been much easier; she, for one, had been younger and besides by the time Inga went away to college, David had moved in…David…

Claire shut her eyes firmly and placed a hand over them. She turned her head to one side, thinking wearily, *I'm headed to 'Frisco today, not the Big Apple or D.C. I'll be on a commercial jet, not a goddamn 1969 Navajo twin engine. Ruth is seventeen, not a child! Love means letting go. You must try harder.*

But her nerves were off on a workout, forcing forward that simple, alarming fact that someday, somehow, she, and all she loved…*won't wear sneakers*, she thought, pushing aside the weight of transience, reaching for the clear-cut, the ordinary, something she could handle. *Better those new black sandals, easy off and on*, and then she rolled over to her side, mildly outraged again, and yet again, by the most recent empty space in the bed where David once had been and where their beloved pup, Buddy, still should have been, his dark Dalmatian eye upon her, his long trim dog's body hogging most of the mattress, unfurling for a belly-rub the moment even just one eye slit open…a week, just a bare week gone. It already felt like forever.

"Bud," she murmured and tugged the comforter around her bare shoulders. Damp from newly habitual night sweats, a bit chilled by the A/C, she shivered and shot a glance up through the skylight into a clear and searing Florida coastal sky, today a seamless and unseemly blue, that Virgin Mary's veil-from-her-childhood blue that made her want to cut a swath of it for a blindfold. She heard Inga in the kitchen, grinding coffee. Ruth was probably still asleep. Claire yawned, and one side of her jaw clicked. She felt exhausted already, as tense as a trip-wire, eyes wide.

"Travel stress," she said aloud, but softly, lest Inga scold her for talking to herself. "Well, what can she expect? I'm fifty— this morning! And living alone with my lovely, crazy-ass teen-ager—" she spoke to the dim room as she took a full body stretch, arms akimbo, pointed toes, yoga breathing to try and slow her tap-dancing heart.

And behind the travel nerves, an obdurate solid lump she'd been hauling around like an emotional tumor, ever since she'd had to put Buddy down. Not exactly depression; she'd battled that for almost two years after Ruth's birth. Postpartum certainly, but there had been so much more, then. No, this bitter weight was different than commoner–garden depression;

it had an angry zap in it, like a late afternoon summer thunderstorm, massed on a Florida horizon, brewing up a tropical storm with ground-sizzling bolts, and she thought *life, after a certain age, is just too much about loss* making her think of Gloria, dwindling daily in hospice, living out a death sentence week by weight-dropping week. Claire shook herself again.

"Stop that—good God," she said to herself. "Get on past it, will you?"

"Mom?" Inga called down the hall. "Are you awake?"

"Coming." Claire pushed aside mortality again, and swung her small, tan feet to the carpet. A clump of Buddy hair clung to a corner of it.

Needs a vacuum, she thought. *Whole place could use a good scrub—*

"Ma—breakfast! We must get out of here by nine if you want to get through security in Jax. It's almost 7:30."

"Hold your dang horses, missy," she murmured, reaching to the end of the bed for her robe. She always slept in the buff and Inga, for some unshared reason, did not approve. Claire chuckled at that, and, peering into the big rectangle of a mirror hung over her dresser, tousled her curly salt-and-pepper-hair into something akin to her usual, casual style, belted the thick-pile blue terry robe around her naked waist, found slippers and sashayed, just because she felt it might lighten her mood, out the bedroom door, two-stepping down the hall and into the sunny kitchen where the air was rich with fresh-ground coffee beans.

"Good morning!"

Inga looked up from the coffee pot on the kitchen island. At thirty-three, she'd become a reserved, squared-shouldered woman with a swan neck, dark, dense hair close cut to her skull and a brown, heart-shaped face. In a glossy crimson silk dressing gown, with pajamas to match, she looked, to her mother's eyes, the epitome of a womanly elegance that she herself had given up on long, long ago.

I may be fifty, Claire thought, *but I still act like a kid, snapping gum, wearing Levi's, a baseball cap and beat-up black hi-tops. Inga, child, if you've got it, flaunt it.*

"'Bout time," said Inga, and stepped over to give Claire a kiss. At five eleven, she had to bend down to her mother's cheek. "Happy birthday."

"Fifty, can you believe?"

"It's just a number." Inga turned her attention to the coffee pot, and pressed the *on* button. "You don't look a day over forty."

Watching her daughter's lithe back, marveling again that so balletic a creature was her own, Claire said, "Thank-you. Make it thirty and I'll leave you all my scientific millions."

"Thirty. But only if I get to be thirty, too."

"Done. We'll both stay thirty forever. Just don't notice the gray."

"I call it silver, not gray. Never gray. But, Ma, you've really got to get a move on!"

"Why? I'm packed, my travel clothes are laid out, all I have to do is eat and jump in the shower. Anyone would think you were the one on the go, not me! So what if I miss the flight? I'd get another."

"Wouldn't that be terrible inconvenience for your friend?"

Claire widened her eyes in astonishment. "Sweetheart, Erin Perlette barely keeps to a schedule, and lives off her cell. I don't think she'd even notice." Claire took a deep breath of the now brewing coffee and opened the door of the refrigerator. "Is Ruth up?"

"That's a joke, right? It isn't even noon yet."

"I figured. Scrambled eggs?"

"Fine. I'll put toast in."

Claire moved about her kitchen of almost twenty years with economy, opening the French double doors to the glass enclosure of her pool, where sunlight, unobstructed, made the water sparkle and dance. She paused, thinking as she did most mornings, *I still can't believe this is mine,* remembering the shame of food stamps and nothing-but-margarine-sand-wiches. She stepped over to a saltwater aquarium and scattered some feed, and then back into the kitchen, to crack eggs and whip them with *Lea & Perrin's,* cream and pepper, a breakfast ritual. She turned on the gas to a moderate flame, chose a skillet hanging above the island.

Inga, watching her mother, asked, "How has work been? You've not said a word about it since I got here, and that's not like you."

Claire frowned and said slowly, "That's because I'm stuck. I thought by the end of last semester we'd be closer to some kind of animal trials, but no. Puerto Rico isn't doing any better. José's experiments with *Holothuria glaberrima*—"

"Translation, please?"

"Sea cucumbers. Echinoderms, like sea-stars."

"Starfish."

"Oh, right, that's right, go ahead, provoke your old mother on her birthday! You know perfectly well sea-stars aren't fish; more properly, they are *asteroidea.* Sea cucumbers have the same regenerative ability as my asteroids. José is interested in wound closure, so he and I have the same problem. I mean, once you get cell growth to start—"

"—how do you do you tell it to stop?" finished Inga.

"Cancer, of course, is the other side of that fence and so I can't stop thinking about Gloria Perkins."

"I'm sorry, Ma. Are you very close to her?"

"Not really but she's a—was a damn good scientist. I respect her work, and the University treated us both badly for years, so we had a common gripe. But I know very little about Gloria's personal life." Claire sighed. "She'd gotten some good results with salamanders, before the cancer took hold, and it just leaves me feeling as if a bunch of us all are racing to the same goal, but we keep tripping over our own feet, and for some of us it's just getting too late—"

"Ma, listen to me: you are only fifty."

"I know. Fifty is the new thirty—like hell."

"Ma—"

"Fuck," Claire muttered low. She looked up and raised her voice. "Let's change the subject. When does Max arrive?"

Inga sighed. "He's got a flight from La Guardia booked for Saturday—he'll rent in Jacksonville then drive down."

"He will be staying through the week, won't he? I'd worry about you and Ruth all by your selves, in this big house—"

"Ma! You guys live in this big house all by your selves—"

"Oh, but Ruth and I haven't been alone. Not until this past week, anyway."

"Ma. Buddy was a *dog.*"

Claire sniffed. "Shows how much you know. A dog? Buddy would be appalled. He wasn't a dog. He was a dude." She turned back to the eggs, her face hard and drained, thinking *I'm sick to death of crying.* She cleared her throat to steady her voice. "You know we miss him as much as if he'd been a person. Max will, too. Each time he visited, I swear Bud gained a pound."

Inga chuckled. "Everybody spoiled that dog rotten."

"His due, nothing more. He ruled this household with an iron paw," Claire said as she divided the eggs and scraped them out onto china plates while Inga added buttered toast, and they both doctored a mug of coffee.

"I miss him, too, you know. So, how's that cyst on your back? Still bothering you?"

"Not really, it's just annoying."

"Can't you have the thing removed?"

Claire rolled her eyes. "I had it drained, but these cysts come back like the living dead. It's not serious. Asthma's serious. This thing's more like a bug-bite."

"Has your asthma been acting up?" asked Inga, with sharp concern.

"No. This new medication is like a miracle—sometimes I don't feel like I ever had asthma." She sighed as they seated themselves at a breakfast table, beside the floor to ceiling kitchen window-wall, which overlooked the pool. "But menopause is no fun. Sometimes, I wake up drenched like I've gone skinny-dipping in my bed." She gave her daughter a meaningful glance. "Growing old sucks."

"No kidding. Creaky-crackly knees, chin hair, nose hair—"

"Oh, please. You're a *child*." Claire stabbed up some eggs with her fork. "Fifty's another ball of wax. Gloria, you know, is fifty-seven but it doesn't look like she's going to make fifty-eight."

"Cancer disrespects age. You're not keeping something from me?"

"Oh, sweetheart, no. I'm just frustrated and feeling, well, old. Both my STINT grant and my sabbatical are about to run out. All these young people in Iraq blown to bits, and if we could only figure out…" she made a fist "—exactly how to translate echinoderm tissue regeneration! We could learn to fix ourselves, grown new limbs!"

Inga smiled indulgently. "And what if we could just grow new everything, when it aged or broke down? New heart, new head, new lungs, new liver, regenerate it all and never die—childbirth would become obsolete."

Claire raised her eyebrows. "Funny, very funny. I do *science*, not science fiction." She mused for a moment. "Still, I want, so want to leave something behind when I'm gone, something I don't know, something fine, something…"

"Aren't me and Ruthie fine enough?" said Inga, miffed.

"Oh, honey, of course. You know what I mean."

"Sure, Mom," said Inga, putting a gentling hand on her mother's agitation. "I don't mean to be abrupt, but I have a birthday present for you."

"Oh, no, I told you and Max to save—"

"Hush, I didn't spend a nickel. I want to give it to you right now: we're expecting. I'm two or so months along. So you see how glad I am science has not made childbirth a thing of the past."

"Oh my—oh my—Inga—" Claire gasped "I—it's just wonderful! Never mind me, I'm just a middle-aged, addle-brained professor—come over here and give your mother a hug!"

Which Inga did. Taking her seat again, she smiled and said, "I'm famished, of course. Scrambled eggs are just the ticket, but I think another slice of toast—"

"Do you want my plate as well? I don't know if I can swallow another bite!"

"You'd better eat. The flight's long and they only throw snacks at you these days—if that. I got *nada* coming down here but an examination of my boots."

"So let me see—you'll be due—"

"October. I'll take a leave of absence from the firm, of course. I may even quit for a spell. Contract law isn't all that interesting in the face of being a mom. We've decided to be old-fashioned and find out the hard way whether it's a boy or a girl."

Claire eyed her daughter's brown-gold face, glowing with her birthday present delivered. "Are you sure you don't have a preference?"

"Did you?"

Claire laughed and took a sip of coffee. "Well, to be quite frank, yes. When I came down off the ceiling from shock to think about just what I was doing, me, not more than a kid myself, I knew I wanted a girl. The second time, too, though I'd never admitted it to David. He wanted a son, in his heart of hearts. So I got lucky, didn't I? Two lovely girls."

"Well, I don't care either way. If we have a boy, we're calling him Nicholas, just because we like the name. A girl—" her brown eyes twinkled— "will be Claire."

"Oh, heavens, don't burden the child—such a solemn name, like an old lady. I wanted to be Jenny."

"Jenny? Ma, there are a thousand and one Jenny's. I'm very glad you didn't do me that honor!"

Claire smiled. "No. I wanted something of your screwed up family heritage for you, so I went with the least likely, the Scandinavian."

"For a half-Danish great-grandmother none of us ever knew."

"And you chose the name Ruth for your own sister, if you'll recall. Remember how surprised your father was?"

Inga nodded, nibbling at her toast. "Yes, I do but I don't see why. Nana Ruth had been very kind to me. But I've always kind of wondered why didn't you go for the Scottish or Irish or German—or even the Cherokee on. Nana Jane's side? That would've been interesting."

"Don't be silly! How would I know a Cherokee name from Adam, me, a Jersey girl? The only kind of Indians I knew were

Cher and Tonto. Besides, I thought Inga sounded regal and I was infatuated with Ingrid Bergman. As for your biological father, I've preferred to leave him out of the picture, for a number of reasons."

"Inga isn't Ingrid and Bergman was a Swede, I might point out, not a Dane."

"Details!" Claire waved her hand as if she wielded a detail-disappearing wand.

Inga smiled. "I thought you scientific types respected details."

Claire huffed. "My Scots-Irish-German-Cherokee and everything but the kitchen sink mother's name is Jane—which is English, so far as I know. And my part-Danish and whatever else was thrown into the mix father's name was Elijah, hardly Danish, but then again, as you just pointed out, he never even knew his mother, poor thing, died when he was still a baby."

"Like my father, dead before I got here."

Claire's face closed up. "David was your father."

Inga cocked her head. "That's true. More than true. My stepfather was a remarkable man and you know I loved him. But I never even met my biological father. At least you remember yours."

"Barely more than cold, stern shadow. Though I do remember—"

"—one happy summer's afternoon on a beach, with your Dad and your dog, hunting mussels. Which is more than I can say."

"Fate," said Claire heavily. "Trust me, sweetheart, I've come to believe you were better off. Your father was a boy when he died, but he would've made a lousy father. Handsome, artistic but not responsible or reliable."

"So it runs in the family, I guess, absence and irresponsibility?"

"Oh, Inga, please. I'm not irresponsible—and neither was my mother."

"Okay, okay. Nana and your father came to hate each other, so they just split. Hard to fathom, just walking away like that; I know I couldn't do it. But I suppose Nana was dead set on what she thought best."

"—you know how Nana gets. And Dad? Maybe there was another woman. Anyway, he was content to let us both go. It was just me and Mom—and then Rags, and you in Jersey. My West Coast childhood got bottled and stowed away. Mom wouldn't talk about it. Now it feels impossibly ancient, as if it happened to someone else."

Inga smiled reminiscently. "Rags was a real clown."

"As only a terrier can be."

Inga stirred herself, and looked up. "Are you sure your father is still alive?"

"No. But I mean to find out for once and for all, on this trip," she said and bit her bottom lip a little, as she turned to gaze out over the winking iridescence of the blue-blue pool. "What a beautiful day it's going to be," she said absently, as something in the other pool, the bleak one in her mind, surged. Her childhood might be as far away from her Florida coastal home as the moon, but it hadn't wholly vanished. Sometimes, she wished it would, rather than trailing after her, as loud and annoying as tin cans tied to the bumper of an old car: a failed marriage, a lost home…she turned back to Inga.

"Do you think about him so much, your father?"

Inga grew still. "No…it's just getting pregnant. Sets one's mind on things generational."

"And genetic?" said Claire. "Are you worried about something in particular?"

Inga shrugged.

"You shouldn't be, not so far as I know. And sweetheart, would you do me a favor and remind Ruth she's got diving practice this afternoon?"

"All right, but she's not likely to forget. She's a fish, that girl."

"Hmm?"

"Nothing." Inga began to drum her well-manicured fingers on the table.

Claire turned back around. "Inga? Something wrong?"

"Nothing's wrong. Not wrong."

"Well then?"

Inga looked up searchingly and said, "Did Ruth tell you she's got a meeting with her coach today?"

"No—why? She's not in trouble, is she?"

Inga shook her head. "No, not trouble, it's just that she's been—oh, never mind."

"Never mind what?"

"No, no it's between me and Ruth." Inga looked up, her face tense. "Listen, Mom, I've got to ask you about this, well, other problem—I guess you could say I am worried about something in particular and I feel, I don't know, silly? Guilty about it—I mean, do you think I should tell Nana about the baby now? Or should I wait until you come back home? I'm nervous. I mean, the way she does still go on about Max. I laughed it off at first, it seemed too ridiculous to complain when our own family gene pool is so mixed up, but she does not let it go, she just doesn't quit. It's so embarrassing. I mean, what if the baby's skin is darker than mine or yours, or has Max's eyes—or both?"

"Then he or she will be beautiful," said Claire, troubled by the pain that had now taken over her daughter's usually open face. She reached out a hand to touch Inga's cheek. "Nana is old and set in her ways. You know how I've been worrying about her. She's grown fretful and petulant—even a little paranoid since I had to put her into assisted living."

"But you had to—" said Inga, folding and unfolding her long thin fingers. "She wasn't taking care of herself."

"I know. Still, she hates the place. She told me she's just plain jealous—why can't she be young and carefree? And what can I say? There's no answer except the obvious. She's past seventy, with rheumatoid arthritis complicated by osteoporosis."

Inga was silent, for she had seen her Nana Jane chastise her mother over little things or nothing at all, heated exchanges that had nothing to do with reality and everything to do with Jane's outrage at being diminished by age.

"Nana has always gotten her way."

"Mostly. She hates being dependent."

"So do you—so would I and if Ruth's bull-headedness is any sign, so would she."

"As I said, getting old sucks. Not for the faint of heart."

"And that's not what I meant. I meant that we are all Nana's girls, aren't we? Ruth has Nana's stubbornness and you sure guard your independence rather fiercely."

Claire regarded her daughter. "Is that a problem for you?"

"No, no, of course not! I'm just saying—"

"Like Nana, like daughter?"

"Well, if I do have a daughter, I'll want her to be her own person, have her own mind. But then again sometimes, I don't know, Mom, I wish you had more friends—or a boyfriend. Get out more."

"I have friends," Claire protested.

"Who? Ruth will go off to college soon—and then what?"

"Well, I don't think I'd be visiting the West Coast to celebrate this dang birthday if I didn't want to see Erin and Noreen, now, would I?"

"I mean *new* friends. Here, in Florida."

"I have colleagues," said Claire, defensively.

"Right. Colleagues—like Gloria Perkins. I mean friends, not lab mates, or grad students. And not your neighbors, either even if they are perfectly nice, as neighbors."

Claire shrugged. "I've always been something of a loner. It's the work."

"I know. But the last man I remember you even mentioning was—"

"Michael, yes, I know. But Michael was insecure. He wanted too much—no, he needed too much and besides, he didn't really like children, and there was Ruth to think of. He was mule-headed, too."

"Max is mule-headed. So am I. We can be like two bulls, horns locked."

"Yes, but you have a sympathy that Mike and I just didn't— the whole thing was a mistake. Besides, that's the past. I want to look forward, to my grandchild—oh, I'm so happy for you and Max—and for me, too, of course. What a lovely birthday gift—"

The phone interrupted. Like most professionals Claire relied on her cell, but still kept two landlines, one in the study, one in her bedroom. "I'll get it," said Inga, waving her mother off. "You hop in the shower, young lady."

"Yes ma'am!" Claire tucked the last corner of toast in her mouth, took her coffee mug and headed back to the bedroom while Inga strode over to the studio/study, where Claire not only kept one of the phones, but also part of her extensive library and an array of assorted paints and crafts. The closer she came to retirement, the more she spent time dabbling in things she'd loved to do as a child—watercolors, embroidery, crocheting—making things, pretty things, useful things, give-away gift things, things she and her mother used to make together. But lately, even this amusement had ceased to inspire.

Claire padded quietly down the hallway toward the bathroom but when she noticed her younger daughter's bedroom door ajar, she couldn't resist peeking in—just to be sure everything was all right. Ruthie lay with her back to the door, a compact ball of teenage muscle not an extra ounce anywhere, a swimmer even in her sleep, with the white sheets pulled up close about her shoulders. Claire listened to her daughter breathe but those sheets conjured a sharp, brief memory of Ruth as a tiny little bit of a baby, dwarfed by a huge, chrome gurney, drowning in white sheets, hooked up to a monitor, sedated and the surgeon's voice, seemingly far off yet reassuring, "it's a small hole in her heart, easy to repair, she will live a normal life—"

Claire turned away and shut the door with a click, forcing herself to forget. She hurried to the bathroom, turned on the shower and threw off her robe with a quick, strong shrug. *What is a normal life?* she asked herself silently, and for the thousandth time. She'd had never wanted just a normal life, she wanted something big, bold—magical.

Claire laughed at herself as she undressed, thankful for the normal after all. *And by the time this new baby will be old enough to play,* she thought adjusting the shower's temperature, *I'll be a doddering old fool, and ready to finger-paint! A grandchild—me, a grandmother!* She soaped and sluiced, humming an old Carole King song, the one she'd played over and over and over again until she thought the wax groove would simply melt, *Will You Still Love Me, Tomorrow?*

Sweet sixteen and more than just kissed, she thought, with a shade of worn out bitterness. *I thought you would still love me, tomorrow, Jordan Valery. Fool that I was.*

Stepping out of the shower, she dried off, slipped back into her robe and toweled her springy hair from wet to damp. She dressed quickly in jeans, grimacing at her weight—*why can't I lose five pounds? Just five!*—and a black t-shirt, slid her feet into her new flat black leather sandals with a big metal O ring—*so retro sixties*, she thought, smiling briefly—and wheeled her suitcase to the kitchen to find Inga sitting at the breakfast table again, both hands cradling her coffee mug, staring out at the window-wall into the flood of Florida sunshine.

"Who was on the phone?" asked Claire. She glanced at her watch. "My God, would you look at the time! You were so right we'll have to hurry—Inga?"

"It was a man. He said his name was—" she paused— "Jordan Valery."

Claire froze. Having conjured with the name in the shower, she was floored to hear it again, so soon and this time spoken aloud, and by Inga of all people. Stung, Claire said, "But that's impossible. Did this…this person say anything else?"

"He said he thought he might've known my father."

"Of all the—that's nonsense. Why would anyone in his right mind call here and use that name, say such a fool thing? Jordan Valery got drunk, took his brother's Beetle for a spin, and wound up DOA nearly forty years ago—"

"Ma—"

"—who in the world would pull such a prank? Was it one of his jailbait cousins? What monsters—but they should leave you out of it! If I catch—" but she had to catch her own breath instead.

"Calm down, Ma, you'll give yourself a stroke. Look, I'm not upset, it just took me by surprise, that's all. The man, whoever he was, only said he thought he might've known my father: past tense. It's probably some mix up. He didn't say he wanted anything, and when I explained you were leaving town, he said he'd call again, after you return. I'm sure it's something we can straighten out later. Otherwise, you'll miss your flight."

"Huh—maybe I should skip it," she said and folded her arms across her chest. "I don't like this. Not one bit. Life spins along quietly until, *wham!* the boom lowers. First poor Gloria, then Bud, then a crank call like that, maybe I should just postpone—"

"Ma, please don't be superstitious."

"Sweetheart, you know that I *am*."

"I know. How you can be a scientist and superstitious, I'll never get. Come on, let's go. Forget about the call, and try to relax."

"Oh, sure, relax!"

"Ma, it was probably just a mistake. You get your things, and I'll start the car."

Claire got off the plane in San Francisco rubber-legged and out of joint—for almost the whole trip she'd sat bolt upright and flinched at every little creak, sure as hell couldn't doze, and brooded on the prank call. And although she'd made this same cross-country trip many times without ill effect back in the eighties when she'd lived, briefly, on the West Coast, now she felt wobbly and unkempt—*never again, she thought, will I make this trip. Not worth it anymore.*

Squinting into the airport chaos wearily she thought *why is it that everyone here looks faintly familiar?* Shaking herself into something like attention, she made her way across the crowd to the BART station, noticing as she went that SFO seemed lost in time compared to the Dallas/Fort Worth terminal, where she'd had an hour's layover. Dallas had seemed Disney-new and bright, sporting a two-story retail village featuring luxuries once upon a time left to New York City's Fifth Avenue, and an eerie, polymer maze or sculpture that emitted 2001-like tones whenever a person stepped on a lighted circle forming the path that wound through it. By contrast, SFO looked shabby, small and tired—as did the BART, to Claire, when she got on a car: dilapidated and tatty, as if it hadn't been refurbished since she'd gone back East. She held on to the pole as the train barreled along to Glen Park, moaning and howling through a tunnel with a weary, worn-out energy.

Stepping out into the weak spring sunshine that was just barely drying up the early fog, Claire was hit with a pang of utter, inexplicable dread so strong her knees nearly buckled. She was supposed to meet her friend Erin Perlette at the Glen Park BART station, and she knew perfectly well Erin would be late, but as she stood trembling there in the bowl of stone that was the station entrance, she felt cut off and forsaken. Wheeling her suitcase over to a low concrete wall, she sat down to catch her breath. In fifteen minutes, she'd call Erin. In the meantime, she phoned Inga, who was—

"—fine, just fine, Ma. Took a nice swim in the pool with Ruth after her practice—she said she'd call you tonight—made myself free with the leftovers for lunch. You know you make the best moo-shoo on the planet."

"In self-defense. I swear, aside from a single restaurant in Philly, there are no good Chinese restaurants left in America. Especially not in Florida, or at least not in or around St. Augustine, they've all been ruined by cornstarch, MSG and delivery—not like when I was a kid and Egg Foo Yung tasted like something."

"Make your friend take you to Chinatown."

"Good idea. Inga, I have to ask—that…man, that prankster didn't call again, did he? The more I think about it, the sicker it seems. Has to be somebody I know or knew, but why—"

"I wish you'd let it go, Ma. It's probably just a mistake, like I said."

"I worry."

"Don't."

Easier said than done, Claire thought a few minutes later as she folded shut her cell. She scanned the street uneasily—still no Erin. Unzipping the outside pocket of her suitcase, she fingered through a couple of file folders, until she found the blank, black moleskin notebook she'd picked up at a Hallmark on a whim, just after Buddy's diagnosis. Opening it, she read the poem she'd inked on the flyleaf, beside her name and the date:

Laurel in the Berkshires

Sea-foam
And coral! Oh, I'll
Climb the great pasture rocks
And dream me mermaid in the sun's
Gold flood.

A.C. 1915

"Have you ever heard of Adelaide Crapsey?" he'd asked her after English class that day, both of them standing awkward in the high school hall. It was the spring of 1972; she was not yet sixteen, a freshman; Jordan Valery, eighteen, was a junior and, well, cool—scary and cool. He was one of the few black boys in her N.J. neighborhood—well, sort of, his mother was white and his father? Kids used to say his Dad just looked like he had a really good tan. Jordan dared to wear his corkscrew hair quite long, like a droopy Afro. Not a big bold one, but still, it was *way*. That, and his leather jacket and the fact that he was so 'artistic' he actually wore clogs—a boy brave enough to wear clogs because he wanted to be a painter—just too cool.

"Crap who?" she said, nervous and hoping to seem, well, cool herself, but thinking *Mom will kill me, for just talking to him—if she finds out, which she won't.*

"Adelaide Crapsey. Obviously not."

"No one's named Adelaide anymore."

"That's not the point."

"What is the point, then?"

He laughed. "Earl told me you'd be difficult. Smarty-pants, you know that's what they call you?"

She hung her head, wishing for the thousandth time she had Peggy Lipton's straight hair to hide behind and not the annoying pile of curls that wouldn't do anything useful. "I can't help it. I'm smart. I like being smart."

"So do I," he said and shrugged. "She was a poet, in like 1911 or something. She didn't write much but what she did write was strange. My Mom likes poetry."

"Oh. Well. I never heard of her. Is it good poetry?"

He frowned which made him look older than a teen. "I don't know, really. She's an acquired taste, I would say."

"Oh? You mean like Gjetost?" He wouldn't make her feel small. Or young. No by golly, she was almost grown up and definitely sophisticated.

"Come again?"

"It's cheese, sweet caramel cheese, from Norway. My Mom likes it for breakfast but if you've never—"

"Ew. Sounds gag-making."

"Like you said, it's an 'acquired taste'. Anyways, you'd think she'd've come up with something better than Crapsey, being a poet and all. Or Adelaide. Mom has a friend named Adelaide and she prefers to be called Dee-Dee. Imagine Dee-Dee as the better name! Adelaide Crapsey! What can a girl do with that?"

"God," he said, as he unfolded a small piece of notebook paper and gave it to her. "Here. This whole conversation is getting to be a drag. Anyway I found this poem and I thought of you."

So long ago now, mused Claire staring down at the poem. She ran a forefinger over a three words: *dream me mermaid,* which brought to mind more high-school poetry, T. S. Eliot's Prufrock—

We have lingered in the chambers of the sea
By sea-girls wreathed with seaweed red and brown.
Until human voices wake us, and we drown.

"Well," said Erin's voice. "I'll just wait until you finish writing the great American novel or whatever it is you're doing. Don't mind me. I got all the time in the world."

Claire looked up into her friend's smiling, freckled face where fine lines had etched themselves into her fair skin, and her black wavy hair now bore a shock of pure white in the front. Blinking herself into the present, she said,

"You are a sight for sore eyes, girl."

"And you! How friggin' long has it been?"

"Too long—I was at the wedding, remember?"

"That long? You still look the same to me—"

"And you."

They were both lying and knew it.

"Are you sure it was my ill-starred wedding—"

"—yes, but let's not dwell. It's too depressing."

"Okay on that cheery note, let's blow this pop stand. My car's parked up the road a bit. And I mean up, you know, up as in San Francisco up. Hope your knees are in better shape than mine! You can hear them click a mile off—"

Always the talker, thought Claire as her friend rattled on about one thing after another, traffic, the parking, the sheer number of Glen Park dogs and kids— "their parents dress them as if a Haight-Ashbury revival is just around the corner, I swear, toddlers who look like Janis Joplin, for friggin' sake. Don't mind the Civic, looks like a rattle-trap but it runs just fine and it's in plenty good shape for the drive up to Portland, I just had my mechanic give it a once over, and besides I don't see the point in buying a new one when most of the time I walk, BART or bike, but you know I just love San Francisco, should've moved here eons ago, but now I'm here I plan to stay. Permanently. I can't believe you left. When are you coming back?"

"Oh, Erin—" Claire sighed as her friend just missed a pothole and corrected to just miss a hydrant. "Not that old tune again. Somewhere along the line, Florida grew on me. Besides, Ruth's a Florida girl, born and raised. I have a nice house with a pool, and I enjoy my work. Despite how stuck I feel at the moment, marine biology still interests me, which is more than I can say for a lot of people our age."

"Tell me about it. Most of my cousins—and you know I have too many to count—are lawyers and bored out of their minds but they have college tuitions and mortgages. How's Inga, by the way?"

Claire smiled broadly. "Pregnant. Can you believe? I'm going to be Grandma Claire in October."

Erin honked the horn and yelped, pissing off pedestrians and especially the guy in the BMW. "Grandma Claire," she said. "Now that sounds weird. How's your mother taking it?"

"You always have your finger on the hot spot, don't you?"

"Uh-huh because it's a no-brainer. Your mother went wiggy when Inga married Max. Something about one set of grandparents hailing from Okinawa?"

"Mom has her…problems with stuff like that. It was a miracle she didn't throw me out on my ear when I told her I was pregnant with Inga, almost a thousand years ago, though she could hardly complain. I mean, *I'm* not really white-white, even if some people think I am." Claire shook her head slowly. "Honestly, I don't know all that Mom thinks, and I was too young, too arrogant, to ask her. She stared at me until I thought I would faint, then said, 'if you are going to have this baby, Claire, you and I have a lot of work to do. I will not see your life ruined. First things first: you will finish high school, no matter how big you get.' And I did. I got big. But I finished high school."

"Wasn't easy."

"No." Claire's tone warned: no more. Not now.

Erin braked at a stoplight. "When's Inga due?"

"October. And Mom doesn't know about it, not yet. Inga just spilled the beans this morning before I left."

"Oh, I see. Happy birthday, Gramma Claire! Believe me, fifty is a fun one."

"Come off it, you're only fifty-two."

"Whatever. Ah, the ole homestead." Erin nosed the car up to a surprisingly empty curb in front of a row of identical wooden houses, with only inches between them and the front doors all smack against the sidewalk, behind a rusted picket grill fence. Erin leaned against her door as she unlocked it because her sixty-odd pound boxer, Lulu, was on the other side—

"Down girl! Come on Lulu, here's Claire, you remember Claire—" who found herself in the dog's embrace, as all three of them squeezed inside a very narrow hall with a mellowed old hardwood floor against which Lulu's toenails clicked and clattered as she jumped around Claire in pure doggy excitement, insanely wagging the docked stump that used to be a puppy's whip-tail.

"She's not a barker," said Claire as she petted the dog to calm her.

"A jumper, yes, a yapper, no. She was just a pup, wasn't she, when you came out to Utah for a visit?"

"Oh, yeah, just a mite smaller than this! She's beautiful."

"She's got a champion in her family, and papers to prove it. I adore boxers. Come to the kitchen, I'll get her a treat and she'll leave us be—"

Claire followed her friend down a short hall, past a master bedroom on her right, a guest bedroom and a bath on the left, then into a combination living-kitchen-dining room that looked out onto a miniscule back porch which then led down to a tiny, lush garden, but the whole place felt cramped to Claire, as if she were a hermit crab stuffed into an outgrown shell. She hadn't known until just that moment how fond and familiar the wide-open windowed expanses of her bright Florida home had become for her.

"Here you go," said Erin reaching a tin of treats off the top of the refrigerator. "Have to keep 'em up high," she explained. "Lulu can find a liver cookie in a haystack."

"So could Bud."

"Yeah, well." For a second, fear flashed over Erin's face, and Claire knew why: Lulu was the same age, or nearly, as Buddy had been.

"You hungry?" Erin asked.

"Starved," Claire replied, glad to let the moment slide. "All I got was a teensy bag of pretzels for lunch. Say, is there a decent Chinese restaurant around here?"

"Sure, and just your luck, in walking distance. Let's get the luggage inside and amble. You do remember I have to work from seven to nine tonight? Good. Tomorrow, we take off—"

"In the morning?"

"Are you *crazy?*"

Claire laughed. "You know I'll be up with the dawn."

"And you know I won't—Ruth must take after me, not you."

"Ruth takes after her father. I used to call him Dracula, afraid of the rising sun."

"Then call me Dracule Two. You can take Lulu for a walk— she'll go to pieces with joy. She whines and noses me, but she can't get me out of bed before ten."

Together they stowed Claire's things and then walked down Church street, past more houses, apartment buildings, across trolley tracks to a tiny produce market, outside of which someone had left a leashed poodle, possessing it's soul in patience, which appalled Claire, *I could never have done that to Buddy!* Finally they reached a house that had been converted into a restaurant and soon Claire became ever more convinced that there were no good Chinese restaurants left in all of America, even if Erin kept on saying how good the food was. Claire begged to differ but didn't, out of politeness.

Over soggy egg-rolls and salty spareribs, Erin asked, "Have you spoken to Nor?"

"Only about the trip—why?"

Erin frowned. "She sounded, what? Reserved the last we spoke. Like she was holding something back."

"As in?"

"Duh, I couldn't say, that's why I'm asking you but if you haven't spoken to her lately, that gets us nowhere it's just that she seemed—not like Norrie on the phone, you know what I'm saying?"

"Kind of. Why don't we call her and ask?"

"Sure—should, since we need to nail down when to meet and all. How 'bout when I get back from work? She'll be working at the library now, won't she? Yeah, she would be. By the way, my parents are looking forward to seeing you again. Honestly."

"Right, me, the bad influence! Your mother seemed positively shocked to see me at your wedding, as if I'd had something to do with setting you and Harry up. There goes Claire, luring you into heaven knows what depravity!"

"Nah, it wasn't about you. Mom was shocked that I was actually tying the knot. With Harry. I've never seen my mother look so out of it, but the whole Navy Seal, built like a tank, yes, ma'am, no ma'am son-in-law threw her way off, even if she'd known Harry forever."

"You keep in touch with him at all?"

Erin shook her head. "No. Best thing—a full break. Anyway, I'm finally seeing someone new. We met at a mixed singles thing and just clicked. We're both divorced, him twice, so we're taking this whatever we have real, real slow. Haven't told my parents, so just keep it under your hat, please. I can't have Mom jumping for joy that her crazy daughter's back in the land of the vaguely liberal. Might not last."

"What's his name?"

"Carl. Carl McQuade—and yes, he's Catholic. Sort of."

"Catholic, schmatholic, what do I care? I didn't press for details."

Erin smiled. "I'll give you as many details as you'd like, maybe more. I'd introduce you, but he's out of town. Might be home later in the week—he's free-lance. But you know, I do believe my parents will like him. If we get that far, I mean."

"And how are your parents, anyway?"

"Getting on. You'll see. So, tell me more about what you've called this fishing expedition as you call it—what the heck are you fishing for?"

"Ah, well—" Claire said, as the waiter served them watery eggplant, limp broccoli and rubbery ginger-shrimp. "You remember I came out West back in the day because I'd lived in Portland as a kid."

"Sure. Your parents split when you were ten, eleven, and your Mom moved to Jersey. Frankly, I can't imagine having to trade Mt. Hood for Hoboken."

"It wasn't Hoboken. Besides, New Jersey is the Garden State."

"My ass. And?"

"At the time I didn't tell you—or anyone else—that I was searching, in a lame way, for my father. I had nothing tangible to go on, a few memories. Mother was outright against it, and would give me no help, except to agree to care for Inga. I was stubborn. I flew off to Portland, got a job, mooned around the city, then crawled up and down the whole coast from Seattle to San Diego living on nothing better than foolish hope. Like perhaps I'd run into him or something?" She shook her head. "Nonsense."

"So *that's* why you kept moving!"

"Yep. Found nothing but hunger. Got troubled by aimlessness, missed my kid, and went back to graduate school. Probably should've been doing that, all along. But now I've come armed with information. If my father is alive, I aim to see him."

"Why? He's ignored you for almost, what, thirty years?"

"Yeah. I want him to tell me *why*."

"Really, I'd think silence says it all but, hey, I'm not you and who am I to talk? I know exactly where my parents are. Sitting down to supper. Pot-roast. Or broiled salmon because Dad's watching his cholesterol. What kind of information do you have, anyway? I assume your mother is still opposed."

"Mom's not in any position to say yes or no."

"Oh. She's that bad?"

Claire sighed. "Her mind is sharp most of the time, but she's in a wheelchair, in pain, and can't really do for herself. Anyway, going through her papers, I found a safe-deposit key and inside the box legal documents. I now have the address of my old house and several other addresses, second or third cousins of Mom's and I thought I'd have another go. Plus the bonus of our reunion, or as Noreen says, 'and the saga of the Three Almost Irish-Catholic Musketeers continues.'"

"Well, then, cheers!" Erin lifted her half-finished beer. "Here's to you, to us, to our road trip and your fishing trip, may we all find a bit of our youth together, and celebrate the fact that we are all still damn here and well enough to do this thing!"

"Amen to that!"

After supper, Erin left for her shift as an evening editor at KQED. Alone in the dark and silence of the little house, Claire unpacked. Lulu's watchful brown eyes kept tabs on her as she unfolded clothes. Then she put another call in to Inga, got the answering machine, so wandered back into the living room, feeling woozy with jet-lag but not yet sleepy enough to crawl into bed, faintly bothered that Ruth hadn't phoned. Erin's laptop beckoned, so she checked in with e-bay, a guilty pleasure; then, on a whim, she brought up Petfinder.com. A colleague at the Whitney Laboratory for Marine Biology had just adopted a cat online, saying it was easier than visiting the shelter because you had less of an urge to rescue very last animal in the place. Once at the website, though, she lacked courage. It was just too soon—Buddy's sharp face and big brown eyes kept flashing out at her, the way he sat beside her still as a tree, the way he exploded down a beach, all muscle and wiry speed in the moment, life itself.

She shut the computer off, left Lulu asleep and snoring on the living room rug and took a shower, which helped—even if the bathroom was a bit more than just untidy. She tiptoed about, not caring to step a full clean sole on the grubby tile floor, *but then Erin has always been a bit of a slob*, she thought. Once dry, she threw a flannel nightshirt over her head, her concession to being a house guest, brushed her hair until her scalp tingled and then went to stretch out on the futon, which despite fresh sheets looked as battered as the BART car. It was lumpy, too, but that mattered little because she practically passed out when her cheek hit the pillow, as if diving fast into the troubled storm waters she'd been brewing inside, deep down below a surface serenity.

Full fathom five, hey, my old man of the sea, Davy Jones locker here I come she hears as she dives to him, back to him in his tomb of a Cessna, making naught but a quiet dream splash, quite unnoticed. Icy waters gripe her skin. Pressure hugs her lungs. She grows a tail. Her eyes strain to find those bright pearls that had been his eyes—iridescent and terrible white orbs in a black and ruined face that make her flip, fish-tail fast, reverse to rising and break to the warm air, floating until a big toe finds sand, her human feet grow back so she can tread the earth again, the sea now no more than a cold foamy slide against her bare ankles. She gets to her feet in the overcast darkness without a star to see by, and staggers to the sandy border beyond the shifting waters, pitch as the Florida night, loud with marsh life, and now she's at the lab, but the dunes and highway that separated the sea from the marsh are gone, smashed and carried piecemeal away by weather; the lab is a shambles, broken glass littered the ground before her, here and there half a test-tube protrudes from the sandier soil—a hurricane's blow. She has to watch her feet, she might cut a sole to shreds, as she tracks back to the beach, away from the human devastation. She turns her naked back to what's left of her lab, out across a heaving sea.

Suddenly, a piece of the night detaches itself from the edge of the water and grows into a shape moving toward her, large, sudden, swift. Had he come, then, had he followed her back from the sea, to life, to land? But the shape isn't running; it's loping, spare and fast. The air turns metallic, sharp and sour, and she springs, terrified, for the water, but the weight of the animal possesses her and then she's jolted out of the nightmare, as all sixty pounds of Lulu heaves up onto the futon. The boxer put her nose to Claire's ear, sniffs, then nudges the nape of the human's damp neck—Claire shivers, drenched. But Lulu doesn't care. She takes a few turns around until settling a long, warm and bony dog's back against the human one, sinking down into the futon, and it is all Claire can do to stifle a heaving sob. The dog sighs. Buoyed up by Lulu's merely being in bed with her, Claire slowly lets out her own breath. Eased moment by moment by the dog's warmth from the dark undertow of her inner tide, she drifts back to sleep.

Chapter Two

Catch

In the summer of 1967, Claire became a mermaid for the very first time. She'd seen real-live ones at Florida's Weeki-Watchee mermaid park, sea creatures with glittering fantails and strange breathing tubes that fascinated her almost as much as the brilliant, rumbling rocket launch her father had insisted they drive over to the Cape to watch. Later, in her teens, she would fall in love with the manatee, courtesy of Jacques Yves-Cousteau's television special, *The Forgotten Mermaids*. Often, she dreamt of being one, of the freedom to wander sea-beds, unconstrained by equipment, at one with the sea.

But it was back in that summer of '67, in the chill shallows of her parents' oval pool, that Claire first grew a long, brown fin strong enough to flip her across the length of it, or let her undulate under the crisp clear water and it was only then that she knew herself to be a thing of beauty, as she was never on dry land. Amphibious, fabulous, the little mermaid lay languorously across the white steps on the shallow end, half in, half out of the glimmering blue, sunning her bare shoulders and tanning her brown face browner, the honey-gold strands of her springy hair lightening, bleached by chlorine and what little sunshine Oregon's summer offered.

Idly she lifted her fin, making wavelets winking until she grew still and so did the waters since no one shared her grotto, just the little mermaid, whose real name was Star, like the dazzling bright orange or plump purple starfish she'd found while hunting for mussels a week or so ago, when her parents had taken the human Claire, on her two clumsy feet, to a beach house at Seal Rock. She knew, she just knew, if her father could catch a glimpse of Star inside clumsy old Claire, he would stop being so absent and cranky. Secretly eyeing her pregnant mother as the barrier to her father's enlightenment, she held resentment under her ribs like an unopened shell, the pearl of her anger growing as the days of the summer passed slowly one by one, much the same, while her mother's belly swelled like an analog to her secret anger. She thought maybe when the baby was born, maybe when she saw the baby in her mother's arms, she might be able to pry open the shell and cast the pearl away—because the baby would make things right again.

"But she was stillborn," said Claire over breakfast. Erin had finally risen that morning, long after Claire and Lulu had returned for what seemed an absolute revelation of an early morning walk, at least to the dog. After a quick shower, she took Claire off to a neighborhood favorite for breakfast, a fast-paced tiny shop-front where eggs any way you wanted them predominated, and the coffee was both plentiful and fresh.

"What has you mother said about it?" she asked, while peppering an egg-white only, Mexicali omelet.

"Not much. I think she blamed herself, though I doubt she'd done anything wrong. Mother was always so careful. She didn't smoke, she didn't drink—the epitome of an upright, downright Catholic lady. Anyhow, for the marriage, it was the last straw."

"Want more coffee? I'll catch the waitress' eye," and Erin turned full around in her chair until the waitress came and poured them both a second cup. "So do you agree with me?" she asked, reaching for pack of Splenda. "Didn't Norrie sound odd last night?"

"I thought she was angry about something, yes."

"There, see?" Erin spun a spoon around and around in the coffee. "What the heck's eating her, I wonder?"

"Whatever it is, maybe she's waiting for us to get there, for a face to face—just how long is this road trip? By the way, this sausage is great."

"Yeah, they make their own here. Roughly twelve hours. I've actually done it by myself couple times, but it's a stretch. With two, it'll be pie. First stop, *Whole Foods*. I refuse to eat disgusting road fare, so we'll to pick up some gourmet goodies. For Lulu also. They've got wheat-free cookies she likes."

"Why not just load up on French-fries and beer?"

"Don't tempt me!" she exclaimed and then laughed. "Weren't those Friday nights fun! Leave the city after work, drive up to Gram's, start the bonfire on the beach, drink beer, eat fresh fries under the most gorgeous night skies, chock a block with stars. You know I've never slept a whole night on a beach with just a blanket and a fire, since then."

"Me neither—though sleeping a whole night tucked safe in my bed has been a problem lately. God, Erin, last night was great. Slept like the dead. It was all Lulu's doing."

Erin laughed. "That and jet lag."

"I'm sure it helped. Anyway, your grandmother was such a special person, not to worry about us out there on her beach, half-drunk, all alone in the dark."

"Grandmother was something else. Besides, she owned most of Arch Cape, and knew the entire coast like the back of her hand. We were safe. I don't know if we'd still be safe, now, sleeping out in the open like that, but we were back then."

"Being under the stars on the beach with you took me home, in a way nothing else ever did. Did I never tell you?"

Erin shook her head. "Not until now. Come on let's get a move on, we have twelve friggin' hours on the road to talk."

An early afternoon sun finally tore through the fog and San Francisco glowed, glass and metal sparkling, as Erin rattled and hoomed the Civic over the Bay Bridge. Claire stared hard at the cityscape she'd left behind in her twenties and yet, being there, in the car, on the road, made her feel as if all the years in between were slowly collapsing, folding up on themselves and vanishing; she wasn't fifty anymore, she was twenty-two.

"Maybe eleven," she found herself saying aloud, looking down at her new eco-sneakers: brown hemp, purple laces. Cool. "What year is this?"

"Hey, don't ask me," said Erin, her gaze concentrated on Bay area traffic. "I'm having trouble with time. Seems like yesterday you, Norrie and me rented the Red House—yesterday, not twenty-some years ago. No, no, don't make me think about it! Would you look at that guy? He must be doing fifteen, if that. Move over, Grandpa!"

Erin drove fast and easy, familiar on this road, native territory, and kept up, as only she could, a running commentary on the state of the State of the Union, the weather, on the necessity of animal rights and euthanasia and how appallingly restricted civil rights had grown, stalled inside the vacuum of the Bush

Administration and couldn't anyone see how the mere fact of Condoleezza Rice had knocked both civil and women's rights back several notches, not to mention being evil, and so on as they glided out past city and suburb into desert-like Northern California hills, dry even in spring which gave way slowly to Oregon green, which Claire knew would grow more and more damply intense, and then the snow-topped, foggy mountains and increasing crowds and clusters of evergreen conifers.

Living in Florida, mused Claire silently, *one forgets mountains.*

Mt. Shasta took her breath away as it slowly hove into view, it's cap blindingly white against the crystal clear blue sky, wreathed with a few audacious puffed clouds, making Claire think of Mt. St. Helen's long ago eruption which had changed forever the oh-so-familiar conical peak she'd known as a child. When she saw Mt. St. Helen's again in '83, it looked as if a giant toddler had mashed down the top with a fist.

"I can feel the temperature dropping," she said.

"Yeah, well, we are seriously climbing now, just listen to this car complain, can you hear her? Groan, groan. How's Lulu?"

"Fine—dreaming of squirrels."

"Wait until we get home! My parents have a couple bird-feeders on the back deck and the squirrels like to raid them—Lulu can hardly wait to get through the sliders at those little buggers, so anxious I'm almost afraid she will go straight through the glass, but no she waits until Dad opens them up and then *bang* but the sound of the lock has alerted the rodent crew and they've high-tailed it out of there before the dog can get on deck."

Laughing at that scenario, Claire said, "Buddy just could not have cared less about squirrels. I don't know why, he acted as if such work was beneath him—better left to the terrier set, like the scrappy little Cairn Mom had when I was a teen."

Erin eyed Claire briefly. "And how are you doing with it? Or without him?"

"Best I can."

"Want to talk about it?"

"No."

Erin sighed. "Good, actually. I don't think I'm up to it. Let's stop here for a pee, okay?" She nodded out the window at the sign REST AREA—1.5 miles and then pulled into the right lane to slow.

When Claire got out of the car, the crisp cool air, drenched with the pungency of pine and cedar, went to her head like Greek retsina wine, acrid and pure and so cleansing it almost, but not quite, blew away the gloom under the back flap of her mind. She threw out her arms and twirled around and took several deep breaths, thinking *how have I lived without this?*

"Come on, lazy girl," said Erin to the dog. "Get up and stretch those legs."

"God I miss these mountains."

Erin grinned. "I would. Don't get me wrong, I am in total love with 'Frisco, like I said, but I do need my Oregon fix now and then. Want to eat?"

"Sounds like a plan."

"Why don't you help yourself while I walk Lulu?"

Claire nodded and as Erin went off with a reluctant, sleepy dog in tow, she popped the trunk and opened the cooler for a roll-up turkey and cheese. She unfolded the wax paper, and watched the dog look for a suitable place to deposit a load.

Claire closed her eyes, still taking in the evergreen air and then had a flash memory: herself with her golden retriever, running together on a trail thick-padded with a layer of copper-colored needles, gulping winter-cold air until she dropped to her knees and buried her face in the dog's haunch, crying, hard. She opened her eyes and frowned, as Erin approached.

"What's up?" she asked.

"I can't quite remember."

"Remember what?"

Claire shook her head. "I used to roam around the woods a lot when I was a kid but I just had a memory of running up a trail, crying. I can't remember why."

"Yelled at your best friend? Lost a toy? Banged your knee—kids are always crying about something."

"Not me. I was—am—a stoic. Now Ruth, she can become a fountain, but Inga's like me—she'd let out one yell, then it take the rest in stride, even when she broke her ankle. Besides, when I was a kid, my best friend was a golden retriever named, unimaginatively, Honey."

Erin shrugged and leaned her hip against the Civic as she adjusted the red scarf she wore around her neck and shoulders. "Personally, I think you could use a good cry."

"Say what?"

"You heard me. If something's up with Norrie, something's also up with you—I can tell. I think you're right, by the way, about Nor—she's got a bee in her bonnet for sure, a walking around something. You? You seem furiously sad, Claire. A powder keg."

"Well, thanks!"

"Hey, don't get all high-horse with me, I've known you too long, we've done too many road trips together, spent too many hours inside one another's head so you can't tell me it's nothing because I know it's there, whatever it is, sitting there behind those big brown eyes, watching, and it's got teeth. Maybe it doesn't want to bite me, but it sure as heck got its trap on you."

"All right!" Claire karate chopped the air between them. "Problem is I don't know what the problem is—might be this fishing trip, but why now? I've been planning it for a year; might be the fact that the lab's gone stale, but that's been true since this last trial fizzled; it might be my age, but as Inga said, fifty is just a number—might be, might be all of these, and still that's not it, and I have to say I'm fed up with it, Erin." She shook her head. "Some days, I'm fed up to here with everything and everybody. Those first days after I put Buddy down, I nearly drowned myself in tears and wine, not at all like me but these past few years have been just too much loss. No, please, no more for awhile at least. Give me a break, God."

"Okay, done. That speech was a start. Feel better?"

Claire blew out a laugh. "Yeah, I guess, a little."

"How long has this been going on, whatever it is?"

"About a year or so, I think, maybe longer—and sure, part of it does have to do with my work. But I didn't use to feel so—sad, you say? I say out of control. Like, I cracked and spilled all over the place when they told me about Bud, I became a raging lunatic at the vet school, screaming 'no! no!' like screaming would make them take it back, unsay 'congestive heart failure'—I—it was embarrassing. I had to apologize."

Erin crouched down on one knee and put her arms around Lulu's neck. "I'd go crazy if something happened to my girl," she said softly. "This dog is my sanity, my life-line, she pulled me out when Harry tried to take us both down."

"Sorry. I thought I didn't want to talk about it, and here I am upsetting you."

"Don't, Claire—don't be sorry." She stood up. "We'll figure it out. As both of our mothers used to say, this too shall pass."

"Maybe."

"Everything passes sooner or later."

"I know," said Claire softly. "That's the problem, isn't it?"

"Oh, brother! Please don't tell me you're going to gloom and doom and think black thoughts of death for the next six hours?" Erin petted the dog's head. "Me and Lu will have to throw you out."

Claire smiled slightly. "No, I promise to lighten up. But there's this, too, someone—some jerk—phoned the house yesterday just before I left to catch my flight and said he was Jordan Valery."

Erin started. "I thought you said that boy died. A long time ago."

"He did. He was all of nineteen in seventy-three."

"What the hell else did the guy say?"

Claire made a helpless shrug. "I didn't answer the phone, Inga did."

"Inga? No wonder you're upset. Now I'm upset."

"Well Inga wasn't, apparently. She thinks it was just a mistake."

"Some mistake."

"Right! But what can I do about it? This man didn't say anything much, and didn't leave a number."

Erin shook her head. "No I guess there's not much you can do—unless he calls back. If he does, read him the riot act and call the police. That's harassment. Come on Lulu, let's get you in the car. Hey, Claire, could you unwrap the other roll-up for me? Thanks." She opened the car door, and Lulu leapt back onto the seat.

"Here you go," said Claire, handing over the sandwich. "Let me drive for awhile? Take my mind off stuff."

"So long as you don't take your mind off the road and plunge us down an overpass! Lulu would not take kindly to that."

It was past ten and dark when the Civic pulled into the Perlette driveway. Erin doused the headlights, turned the car off, and said, quietly, "They've only lived here for two years, so I'm not quite used to this place yet. Mom said she'd leave a key under the mat, and not to worry, we'd have to be a herd of elephants to wake them, they're both sound sleepers."

But Claire made as little noise as she could as she followed Erin up the brick path to the door, and felt like a teenager trying to sneak home past curfew and with good reason: Erin's parents had been very strict Catholics and, eons ago, suspected Claire of sneaking a joint into their home, so when Jack Perlette called her an addict, she turned on her heel and left. When Erin got back to the Red House a few hours later, she claimed she'd managed to explain, but after that incident, Claire always felt watched in the Perlette home. Besides, Kathleen Perlette was a formidable woman, tall, forceful and devout; she had what Erin called "standards" and Claire hadn't made the grade, at least not back in the day.

The Perlette house in the Raleigh Hills section of town was quiet, the wide, gracious living room full of dusky antique furniture shrouded in the twilight of a single lamp left on, the formal dining room in complete darkness behind heavy drapes. Lulu made a beeline down a short hall to a water dish in the kitchen, as Erin led Claire up carpeted stairs, past the closed doors of the master bedroom, to a small guestroom someone also used as a makeshift office.

"Bathroom's second door to the right, my room's first door," Erin whispered. "Need anything?"

"Sleep."

"Yeah, me too. See you in the a.m. Mom and Dad get up early, so you'll have company. And don't worry. They really do want to see you." She gave Claire a quick kiss and closed the bedroom door behind her.

Left alone and without talk for the first time in over twelve hours, Claire felt the silence like a benediction. She sat down on the small double bed, thinking, *I haven't slept on one of these since I left grad school.* Someone—Kathleen Perlette no doubt—had arranged a vase of daisies on the small nightstand and had turned the bed down, leaving a folded Pendleton wool blanket at the foot for extra measure. Claire thought she'd almost never seen a strange bed look so inviting.

But by the time she'd finished in the bathroom and had tucked herself under the blanket, she was so wide awake she thought she might as well dispense with the formality of pretending to sleep, and start making coffee. The whole house was dead still. She rose on one elbow and looked at her watch. 12:30; the next time she looked, it was 1:30. The next time she looked the room had grown larger, and the house—why, she knew this house from some when, and suddenly she was downstairs in a massive stone kitchen out of the middle ages, and there was a party going on, at least that's what it looked like because Inga was helping Ruth frost a cake—

"Claire," said Nana, who was sitting in her wicker rocker, the one she'd inherited from her own grandmother, "come here and help me with this, would you?"

"What is it?"

"I don't rightly know, but I got to do something about it—"

Claire looked into the two-handled basket her mother held out and saw twisted, shiny balls of black, glossy yarn. She put out a hand to touch the yarn, when a length of it reared like a cobra might and wrapped itself like live wire around Claire's wrist—

"No!" she cried, jerking awake and rolling over, straight out of the small, unfamiliar bed with a thunk to the floor, thinking, *where am I?*

Sun streamed into the room through the only window beyond the foot of the bed. Behind the closed door, she heard murmuring, which soon died down and by then she remembered where she was and why. Stiff, she got up off the floor to look at her watch on the nightstand: 8:30 a.m. Laying back in bed, she took a deep breath and then rose to shower and dress. Opening the door to the bedroom with caution, she peeked out. The hallway was empty, all the other doors closed. She took the towels Erin had left on a chair with her across the hall, knocked on the bathroom door, and getting no answer, stepped inside, locked the door and sighed with relief. She hadn't seen Kathleen or Jack Perlette since Erin's wedding, but hadn't really seen them, not to speak to at any length, for about twenty years, and here she was, more or less a stranger, interrupting their breakfast.

"We're all adults now," she said to herself as she dried her hair. Everything from floor to fixtures in this bathroom almost gleamed with cleanliness—not at all like Erin's place. *And maybe all this spic and span is why*, she thought, dawdling. She eyed herself in the mirror: a slightly weathered oval face just beginning to show a second chin—*when did that happen? Got to nip that in the bud. Just five pounds would help. Okay no more chocolate*—a wet mass of salf-and-pepper curls, a few laugh lines and few more worry wrinkles, a mole on her temple, brown eyes that didn't need reading glasses yet: an ordinary, somewhat overweight, going through the change of life, fifty-year old woman.

But she had never, ever wanted to be ordinary, had she?

I want to be—I wanted to be—

"What do I want to be, besides me, Claire Holt: teacher, scientist, mother," she said to her reflection. "Certainly not a twenty-year old sometime vagrant again, for goodness sake. Surely I'll pass muster now?" thinking, *Kathleen Perlette has to be in her seventies and Jack might even be eighty, so why am I so nervous? This is ridiculous. I haven't done anything wrong. I didn't do anything wrong, there was no joint, we'd made that bonfire with cedar and I guess our clothes might have smelled a little like pot—*

"Stop it," she said. "Grow up."

But she still felt the old guilt as she made her way downstairs, quiet and slow; at the foot of the staircase, she hesitated, listening to the silence. But soon the aroma of coffee began to overwhelm her nerves—she wanted a cup, badly. With her heart beating a hard tom-tom, she stiffened her spine for Judgment Day and marched down the hall and into the kitchen—or rather one side of the large room, she saw entering, was kitchen, the other side more like a rec-room, with leather couches before a fireplace and a flat-screen TV.

"Good morning, Claire!" said a white-haired, tiny woman, who stood beside the sink. Claire could barely recognize her as the once-formidable Kathleen Perlette. "It's a pleasure to see you again, dear."

"And you," Claire replied, her mouth dry. "Mrs. Perlette."

Turning toward a big, rough-hewn table that marked the separation of the one room into two, she said, "Jack, you remember Claire Holt?"

Seated at the head of the table, halfies on the end of his sharp nose, Jack Perlette peered over the top of his newspaper. "Yes indeedy do," he said. "Long time, no see, eh?"

She laughed. "You could say that, yes—"

"And how are your daughters doing?"

"Wonderful! Thanks so much for asking. Ruth's finishing high school, and Inga's going to have a baby in October."

"A baby—" Kathleen's very light blue eyes went cloudy. "But she's so young!"

Claire cocked her head. "Beg pardon?"

"Kathy, dear," said Jack in a slight reproving tone. "Inga must be in her thirties by now—isn't that right, Claire?"

"Thirty-three."

"Oh my," said Kathleen, flustered. "Where have my manners gone to? It's just, well, it just doesn't feel that long. Does it, Jack?"

"I keep saying the years flow by like water. Torture." He grinned. "Coffee's made, so help yourself. We go through a couple of pots. Don't be shy."

"Thanks, I could really use a cup."

"And how was the trip?"

Claire chose a flowered mug from a tree of them on the sideboard. "Fine—fun, actually. I haven't done a road trip like that in years. I admit, though, I feel a little sore this morning, sitting all those hours in the car."

"Couldn't do it," said Jack, folding up his paper. "Not with my back the way it is—well," he stood. "You girls let us know what you've got planned—and don't mind us old folks, just go about your business. Kathy volunteers at the hospital this morning, and I'm off to price computers—you saw the old clunker in the bedroom? Gotta get a new one before that one shows me the blue screen of death."

Just then Lulu came bounding across the room to the sliders, and as Erin had said, stood at boxer attention until Jack opened the door and then, bam, out onto the deck, scattering all the red squirrels gathered to thieve from the bird feeders.

Jack chuckled. "You'll never get one, Lulu. Damn things are too fast."

Cold, pine-spiked air filled the room, mingling with coffee, and bacon, frying, then toast as Kathleen got breakfast. Claire took her mug and followed Lulu out to the deck, which was far higher from the sloping earth below than she'd thought—the house had been built on a ledge over a sharp decline into a forested lot. A set of wooden stairs zigzagged to the stones below and onto a pristine carpet of lawn. A thriving vegetable garden ran along a high wooden fence on one side of the yard; over top of it she could see neighbors, whose deck was built in the same fashion as the Perlette's, eye level. The neighbor smiled and nodded.

Lulu bounded back up the stairs from the yard to snuffle Claire's hand.

"Looking for treats," said Jack from the doorway.

"Sorry, girl, I don't have anything. This is a lovely place, Mr. Perlette."

"Jack, please, and thank you. We fell in love with it first time we saw it and haven't regretted buying it. Anyway with all the grandchildren, we needed more room. Both of Erin's sisters have four, five boys and three girls, and there's Lulu, of course."

"Honey?"

"Yes, dear?"

"I'm off. Remind Erin that I'll be at the hospital till noon."

"Will do," he said, turning back to the dog, who was leaning her handsome brown and white head against his leg. "Come here, girl, Pop'll get you a treat."

Claire smiled. "You're a lucky girl, Lulu."

"Good morning, Pop," said Erin, giving her father a kiss.

"Muffin, it's so good to see you—" he hugged his oldest hard.

"Where's Mom?"

"Gone off to the hospital—you must have just missed her, I think I hear the garage door closing. I'm sure she left breakfast for you."

"I told her not to."

"Right, so you'll find it in the oven, keeping warm. I've got to go computer shopping, so you girls let us know what you've got planned—"

"For starters, we will make dinner tonight, all right? Tell Mother. Or I'll phone, after breakfast. You remember Noreen Brennan? I've invited her over for dinner."

"You did?" asked Claire.

"Just now—caught her before she left for work."

Jack nodded. "Yes I know Noreen. Her boys do yard work for us, summers."

"Really?" said Erin. "Nobody told me! She'll be over around six. In the meantime, Claire and I have some sleuthing to do."

"Sleuthing?"

"Tell you over dinner. How does pike sound?"

"Like fish. Make sure it's fresh."

"Come on, Pop, do I look like a sucker?"

Jack laughed, and walked over to the cupboard, got a chew for Lulu and said, "Well I'm off. Don't get into any trouble."

"Trouble is my middle name," said Erin, yawning. "Come on inside, Claire, and get some grub. Mom can't stop herself from being my Mom, can she? I told her we could get something on our own." She shook her head.

After breakfast, Erin found a city map, and located the address of Claire's old home—which was almost exactly as Claire remembered it, some forty odd years ago, when architecture either went space-age or vaguely Asian; the house had a high peaked roof, and front double doors painted bright red with two elaborate round brass handles and one lone, high and narrow window breaking the timbered wall that overlooked a yard full of leafy greens, a garden of various flowering and fragrant plants and shrubs. A winding slate path ran from the sidewalk to the stoop.

They sat in the car for a few moments, staring at the bright front door.

"There was a pool in back," said Claire. "Wonder if that's still there."

"Seriously, it looks the same?"

"Almost. We had a conventional lawn. Dad mowed it with a manual."

"A push mower?"

"Yep."

"What do you want to do?"

"Knock."

"Seriously?"

"Erin, why do you think I came all the way out here? Just to stare at closed doors? Maybe the people who live here remember my Dad. Maybe they bought the house from him. Who knows? I won't if I don't knock. You can stay in the car if you want."

"And miss the drama—no way. It's just, well, they're complete strangers."

"You don't talk to complete strangers in your line of work?"

"All right, let's do it."

The two women opened the car doors simultaneously, as if on some stage cue. Erin locked up, as Claire made her way to the walk, feeling the eerie monster of time bearing down. She'd dashed through a sprinkler in this yard, and buried a jay that had broken its neck flying into a window in the back. Even though the garden was as new as the slate walk, the whole place felt like a house out of the past, at least for Claire. With Erin at her side anchoring her to the present, she rang the doorbell.

A tall black woman, with a short, severe haircut just graying at the temples answered the ring. "Good morning," she said, questioningly. "I'm afraid if you're selling—"

"No, ma'am," said Erin, overcome by a Catholic-school politeness that surfaced, but rarely. "We're not selling anything."

"Excuse me," Claire cut in. "I'm sorry, I—I used to live here. A long time ago."

The woman smiled graciously. "Oh, really? When?"

"In the early sixties. My name is Claire Holt, and this is my friend, Erin Perlette."

"I'm Mrs. Green. Debra Green. My husband would know more about the house—it was his, before we married. Eli?" she called over her shoulder. "Elijah!"

Claire felt all the blood sink down to her heels but before she could prepare herself, her father, in the flesh, big as life, stood in the doorway, a broad-shouldered man grown a bit stooped, heavier than she remembered, wearing glasses she'd never seen him wear and with a head of pure white hair but still, it was him, her father. Elijah Green. He regarded his daughter without surprise from behind his round tortoise shells.

"Well, I'll be. It's Claire," he said in a mild, deep voice so familiar it made Claire shrink into a child. His voice hadn't changed at all.

"You know each other?" said Mrs. Green with incredulity.

"I should. This is my daughter, Claire." He folded his arms meditatively. "Although I haven't seen her since she was—what, eleven? Eleven or twelve."

"Ten," Claire managed to squeak.

Without moving, Eli Green closed his eyes and blew out a sigh. Opening his eyes, he said, "I'll need some time."

"But I want—I'd like to talk to you," she said, then paused. "Dad?"

"Eli, what is going on?" asked Mrs. Green, glaring at Claire now with blank astonishment and something else, something that came out in a minute as, "I don't understand. This woman is—well, she's white!"

Elijah shook his head slowly, and said, "Claire may look white, she may have grown up white, but she is also my daughter.

This is just too, er, serious to hash out in a doorway, wouldn't you say? Claire? Why don't you—and your friend?—why don't you come back tomorrow. Say for Sunday brunch? Give us all a little time. Come on, Debra, I'll explain. Good-bye. We'll see you tomorrow," and then he just closed the door.

A few dead minutes passed until Erin said, "Claire? Are you okay?"

"Okay? Okay?" she replied, with fury. "Of course not. Let's get out of here before I start to scream or pound on the damn door." She marched back up the slate path, shaking, and it took more than several minutes of them in the car crawling back down a winding Northwest street before she was able to say,

"What did he mean, I probably grew up white?"

"That's what the man said."

Claire shook her head. "There's Creole on Mother's side. Is that what he meant?"

Erin shrugged. "How should I know? I think he was talking about himself."

"Himself? Did he look *black* to you?"

Erin shrugged harder, keeping her eyes pinned to the road. "His wife was black, anyway," she muttered. "I mean African-American."

"So?"

"So nothing. I'm just saying."

Claire brooded and then said, "Grew up white? Of course I grew up white! My birth certificate reads color or race, white."

"Well," said Erin tentatively. "You did mention Creole. And Cherokee—"

"Cherokee?" Claire laughed one hard *ha*. "Please. In something like 1800 my mother's grandmother's Scots-Irish-German father married a woman who was Irish-German-Cherokee, which hardly counts, I think."

"Okay, okay! Obviously your parents had race issues."

"They had issues, all right, and if Dad is black, they had much larger issues than Mom ever let on." Claire yanked her cell phone out of her purse and speed-dialed the assisted living facility.

"Mom?"

"Hello, darling, how nice of you to call. When are you coming over for a visit?"

"Mom, I'm in Oregon."

"Oregon? Don't be silly, darling, you can't be in Oregon—"

"Mom, I told you, I've come to visit Erin and Noreen."

"Who?"

"Ma—you remember Erin Perlette and Noreen—"

"You don't come to see me," Jane whined. "And yet you fly off to the ends of the earth for strangers you haven't seen in umpty-ump years? When are you—"

"Mom, listen to me. I've just seen Dad."

There was a mortal silence on the line, then a click and the death of a disconnected line. Claire swore, folded and unfolded the phone to speed-dial Inga but before it rang, she stopped the call and put the phone away thoughtfully.

"Clammed up?" said Erin as she steered the Civic into a grocery-store lot.

"Yeah. I was going call Inga, but I'd better get to the bottom of this first."

"Absolutely. I thought we'd stop in here," she nodded at the store, "buy the makings for dinner. There's not much more we can do about it, now, is there? Unless you want to look up one of those other addresses?"

Claire stared blindly out the windshield, seeing in her mind's eye her father as she remembered him, a thin, tall man with cropped and wavy hair, without glasses and, well, not black, not so far as she'd ever known or understood.

But what did she know? She'd only been ten, old enough to feel the loss of him, but young enough not to understand certain things, maybe certain hushed up or buried things—facts? She dragged herself back into the present.

"No," she said to Erin. "Haven't the stomach for it."

The Three A Wee-bit, Not Quite Irish-Catholic Musketeers—Noreen Cullen, Erin Perlette and Claire Holt—met in 1983, under the auspices of the *Portland Standard*, a left-leaning investigative newssheet, a leftover from the 1960s. They all worked in the production department: Noreen laid out ads, Erin copy-edited and Claire both proof-read and did data entry, being the only one of them, at that time, with any computer experience. A week after their first meeting, Claire moved in with Norrie and Erin, to share a cavernous old Victorian rental in Northwest Portland they dubbed The Red House. The roof sported moss, and the house had no insulation to speak of, so the damp, chill Oregon weather was a problem, but they had their own space, not a childhood home and not a dorm. Claire splurged on an electric blanket. Norrie contracted a head cold that lasted all winter, and Erin periodically went absent to spend the night with her parents, often merely to get a decent meal, or at least not a vegetarian one.

"Poor years," said Noreen, seated at the formal dining table at the Perlette's. Though tall still, the once willowy blond, Noreen Cullen-Brennan, was, at fifty-seven, stout. Her hair had faded to a color that wasn't one, and Claire felt tiny, by comparison. She wasn't sure she would've recognized Noreen, on the street; at table, with friends, yes—but out of context? Claire frowned. Noreen looked—well, old.

"We had fun, though," said Erin. "Even if we were starving."

"It wasn't that bad," Claire protested.

"So say you."

Noreen shook her head. "We were all thin as rails. Claire used to make something called spaghetti squash casserole—you remember?"

Erin laughed. "I'd like to forget it."

"Come on," said Claire. "It wasn't that bad! I still have my Molly Katzen Moosewood cookbook, and I still make it from time to time."

"You don't," said Erin, feigning horror.

"I do. Ruth happens to be fond of it."

Kathleen Perlette looked perplexed, "I've never heard of spaghetti squash."

"More wine anyone?" asked Jack. He stood up and started filling glasses. "How're the boys, Noreen?"

"Fine. Joshua starts his freshman year of college in the fall. Calvin's major occupation these days is mountain-biking, and Matt takes after me: he's a pianist. I think he's going to be a good pianist."

"College," said Claire. "Seems like yesterday I held baby Josh in my arms."

"Doesn't seem like yesterday to me," said Noreen. "Hardly. I love my sons, but raising three boys takes all the stuffing out of you." She smiled, a bit grimly. "And you're going to be a grandmother, Claire. Now *that* seems impossible."

"Exactly." Kathleen nodded vigorously. "I mean it's too young. Too young to have a child." She narrowed her eyes. "Sixteen. Where are the girl's parents, that's what I'd like to know—"

"Mom," said Erin into the sudden silence. "Come on into the kitchen with me for a minute, would you? I need your opinion on the dessert. Dad?"

Jack stood up abruptly.

"Of course I'll help, dear," said Kathleen, sounding mildly offended.

Erin took her mother by the hand, and the Perlette family left a surprised Claire, and a dour Noreen, alone at the table.

"What just happened?"

Noreen sighed. "Memory problems. And too much wine, I suspect."

"But we only had the one bottle between five of us!"

"I know but it affects her more strongly now." Noreen shook her head. "Erin said they tried full-family sobriety, everyone dry, but that made nobody happy. I say, if someone wants to drink, they're going to drink."

Claire gave her friend an inquiring look. "That's sounds like experience."

Noreen smiled bleakly. "I've tried to hide Jim's problem from the boys, but it's gotten worse in the last two years. I've talked to our priest. I go to AA meetings, for the support. Jim won't. I—I'm thinking about divorce. But that would kill my parents."

"Oh, Norrie, I'm sorry—"

Erin walked back into the room. "Let's go to *Rimsky-Korsakoffee*. Or maybe *Huber's*, for Spanish coffee."

"Spanish coffee," mused Claire. "Haven't thought of that in years. God, how it hit the spot after we'd put the paper to bed."

Noreen stood. "Will your Mom be all right?"

"Yeah, Dad'll take care of her. She just gets confused, loses herself, loses track."

"I know how that goes," said Claire. "My mother has lost lots of track. On purpose, sometimes, it seems."

"Yeah," said Erin, heavily. "We three musketeers need to let our hair down like we used to, back in the day of The Red House. Seems to be an awful lot of hair to let down, if you ask me—I heard what you said about divorce, Nor. And me and Claire, well, we had quite the adventure today, didn't we? Scheduled for more tomorrow."

"I think tomorrow, Erin, maybe I should go it alone?"

Noreen looked from one to the other of her friends. "What adventure?"

Erin folded her arms. "I think a flaming carafe of Spanish coffee under the arched stained-glass skylight, stashed away in amongst all that dark, solid mahogany wood is in order. Let's get out of here."

"Your mother was quite a catch," said Eli Green softly. "That's what we used to say in those days. A catch."

Claire shifted uncomfortably. Her back hurt in an odd way, and the couch in the dim living room of her childhood home was hard as a rock. Besides, if years had dropped away when she and Erin left San Francisco, now she felt that time had lost all its meaning or had gained a load of insane meaning she couldn't quite understand: she could not remember this room as distinctly as she would have liked, but knew it nevertheless, and that irritating tick-ticking of the antique clocks her father liked to collect, each one keeping it's own rhythm, no two alike, and that table beside her father's wing-backed chair, and the chair, too, although it had been re-upholstered, a light green chair that had once been dark gold. The several paintings on the walls she knew as his—he'd liked to dabble, and kept a small studio in an extra bedroom, thus her own liking for watercolor. After a short preliminary polite talk, Mrs. Green—Debra—had taken her tea, and gone out, silently, to sit on the porch near the pool where, once upon a time, Claire had become one summer's angry mermaid.

Eli picked up a manila envelope off the coffee table, opened it, and handed his daughter a small, square waffled-edged black and white snap-shot, taken in a booth. "She was so beautiful. The most beautiful creature I'd ever seen, back then."

Claire regarded her mother's face, as it had been some fifty odd years before—an oval-shaped face that she'd inherited. Jane had worn her hair shoulder-length, curled in long, permanent-managed loops as the fifties demanded—*or did she, part Creole, need a flattening iron and relaxer to get those careful curls?* wondered Claire. Jane had a sharp, daring look in her dark, almond eyes, dark lipstick, no doubt a stunning red, and a string of startling white pearls, wedding pearls, the same string Claire had worn, last holiday season. Her mother had given them to her when she'd turned thirty.

"I saved some things, for you, if you ever found your way back to my door," said Eli. He shook the contents of the envelope out on the table. "Our marriage license," he said. "A few more photographs—you can have them—your baby hospital bracelet, and a little baby book your mother kept." He sighed. "How is Jane?"

"Not very well."

He shook his head. "I'm sorry to hear that."

"Are you? Why?"

He stood up sharply and clasped his hands behind his back. "You have every right to be upset, Claire, but your mother and I made some hard choices. We did what we thought was right, at the time." He started to pace. "We'd both been passing, you see. Once we married, we became white. But when we met, we were black. Negro was the proper word, then, the polite word. Or Colored. I was an intern at the hospital where Jane's grandmother was a nurse. Jane and I met at a holiday party. She was, as I just said, the most beautiful creature I'd ever seen—wild, young, angry and ready to take off, so we did, together, we eloped, left Alabama and our past in the dust. We moved to Harlem, and then out here, where Jane had some distant, white cousins and we just passed, the both of us. We could, especially out here—if anybody ever asked, we'd say something about Mexico or Spain."

"*Both* of you?" said Claire, grasping the edge of the couch. "Is that what you meant, then? You're black? You're *both* black?"

"Well, it's complicated, isn't it? I was raised in the South as a colored boy, a Negro. That was the way I was raised. So was Jane. But the two of us could pass easily." He shook his head. "You know how it can work, don't you, Claire? People say, 'he does or doesn't sound black' or 'are they black enough?' in these days. Black power and black pride may not have changed everything but it changed a lot. When I was young, if you were light-skinned but born black, you might choose to pass for white."

"Wait, now, wait. I know Mom said there was Creole and Cherokee in her family, but I took her to mean a century ago or more—"

"Oh, no, not so long, Claire. Your mother's maternal grandmother—she was a nurse—was from Louisiana and she may have said Creole, but she was African, too, with Scots-Irish and German and even a bit of French somewhere; it was Jane's father who had a Cherokee ancestor."

"That, I knew. But Gran Martha? I never met her—"

He chuckled. "Martha Holt was very high yellow, as they said in those days, but she was legally a Negro. So, Jane kept the Cherokee and the Creole, ditched the African? I'm not surprised. When your mother left me, it was 1967. Racial tensions were hotter than hell, and I'd had it with passing. It was time to step up to the plate, and remember myself, my family.

I was a doctor. I could go back to the South and do some good, more good than staying where I was. There was hope in the air, something I'd never really felt before, and I wanted part of it. But Jane said she'd tasted the freedom of being white, and wasn't going back—and she wouldn't drag you to Jim Crow either. I said, Jim Crow is about to die. She said so what, no one would ever make her a Negro again and I said 'you are Negro' and that's when she spat in my face. That was just before she lost our second child." He sighed. "I've often thought about that baby. If she'd lived, maybe things would have been different. She was our litmus test." He touched his chin, his eyes focused on the past. "Jane and I had been rubbing each other the wrong way for a few years, and sparks were flying. When she told me she was pregnant, she was in a state—of panic. What if this child was dark? What if he or she couldn't pass, as we did, as you could pass? What then? Jane was wild for an abortion—"

"Wasn't that illegal?"

He shrugged. "I'm a doctor."

"You would've aborted your own child?" she whispered.

He frowned. "Really, Claire—I'm not a monster. All I'm saying is that we could've found a way, I had friends, contacts, and Mexico was usually the option, back then. But Jane was Catholic, after all, and I wanted the baby. We made a deal. If the baby looked white, we'd stay in Oregon, go on passing and make the marriage work. If the baby was Negro—black I mean—then we'd move back home to Alabama, start over as the black family we should have been all along."

Claire stared at the floor. "When I was a kid," she said at last, "I thought the baby would make you love me again."

"Ah, but I've always loved you, Claire. I never stopped loving my girl."

"Forgive me for saying so, but that's been rather hard to discern," she said drily, the old pain etched in every word.

He winced. "Yes—I didn't—I wasn't happy about it. And I'm sorry. Really I am, especially now after all these years, and the way—life, things, have changed. What we saw as normal, back then, is not, now. And your mother didn't want to change, or rather, she didn't want anything of the past. As a part of the divorce settlement, she took sole custody and made me promise to stay away, to leave you in peace. And I did. I kept my promise. Those first few years were tough. I found out my father had died, and the twins—my brothers—were so angry with me, they cut me off. Only Claire, my older sister, who you were named after, wanted me back but then I found I couldn't do it—move back to the South. I loved—I love—Portland. But here, in oh-so-white Portland, I lost friends, and credibility—and you. Until I met Debra, I was a wreck. Slowly, the tide turned, like I said, things changed. But by the time I got myself in order, so many years had gone I thought it best to keep my silence. I didn't want to cross Jane. In a way, I still loved her—or at least I understood why she went on passing and gave you what she saw as the best chance in life." He sat back in the wing chair, and regarded his daughter steadily. "Does it matter to you?"

"What a question, of course it does, I loved you, Daddy," said Claire automatically. Then she frowned. "What, that I'm not what you just said, oh-so-white? No—and yes. On some level, I feel, what, robbed? I'm fifty years old, and I've spent my whole life as a white woman, so that's what I am, I guess. And besides, how could I possibly mind? My eldest daughter's father was black. Partly, anyway."

"Your daughter? I have a granddaughter?"

Claire smiled sadly. "You have two, in fact, Dad. Inga, my eldest, just turned thirty-three and her half-sister, Ruth, is seventeen."

"So grown," he murmured, shaking his head.

"Oh, Dad!" Claire broke out. "I loved you so, so much! When we moved East, I was heartbroken, and guilty. For years I thought it had to have been me, something about me, that drove you away."

"Oh, no. No, it wasn't—you see that, now? I loved you."

Claire stood up. "How cruel, then, to leave me in limbo."

"Don't say that. Please. I did what I thought was best."

"For you, perhaps. For Mom, even. Not for me."

"Is it too late, then?"

"I don't know." She shook her head, her throat tight. She felt as if she might either contract into a fetal ball or fly apart. "I'm not sure what I want, to be honest. What does your wife think?"

His gaze wandered toward the sliding glass door Debra had taken to the porch. "She knew I was divorced when we married, but not that I had a child." He clasped his hands together tight. "She said the same thing you just did. She's not sure how to feel. I don't blame her—or you, Claire. Your mother and I made decisions. I'll have to live out the consequences."

You'll have to? Claire thought. *What about the rest of us? What about your wife?* Searching or something to break the silence, she said, "Well, you are also going to have a great-grandchild, this winter."

His gaze snapped back to her. "A great grandchild?" he echoed.

She nodded. "My eldest and her husband are expecting."

He looked as dazed as she felt, as he said, "When did you get married, Claire?"

"Married? Married! Oh, dear, that's kind of a funny question. I never had the chance or the choice to marry Inga's father.

And, now, I'm a single mother. But let's not go into that, I just can't—I lost my only real partner when Ruth was ten, and today, well, think I've had enough. Besides which your wife is sitting out there all alone with her thoughts. That can't be entirely good."

"Claire."

"What?"

"I honestly—your mother and I did what we thought best."

Claire almost laughed. Struggling with her temper she said softly, "Sure."

Chapter Three

Little Wounds

At the foot of Mt. Tabor in Southeast Portland, just inside the
park boundary, Erin and Claire met Noreen in the parking
lot for an afternoon hike. Shaken, uncertain, breasting an in-
ternal combustion that had only magnified the dark weight of
conflict she'd carried across the country with her, Claire followed Noreen, following Erin, to the nearest trail, and under
the thick, dank canopy of trees gave her two oldest friends a
very brief, dry account of her conversation with her father. Off
leash, Lulu kept within sight but took the lead as the well-used,
wide path began a fairly steep assent, cutting sharply upward.
The canopy was so heavy and low, it produced a kind of inti-
mate, muffling silence, as if they'd entered a church—Claire
self-consciously lowered her voice.

A sudden view notch that broke showed a snatch of downtown—then, off in the distance, sugar-coned Mt. Hood. Claire
had another flash memory: sitting on the carpet of needles
with Honey panting quietly at her side. She remembered now
that she'd overheard something—*what had it been—what—*

"What are you going tell the girls?" asked Erin, breaking in on the memory. "Hey, there, Lulu, wait for your mom!"

"I imagine," Noreen cut in, "the truth. They have a right to know, especially if Inga's about to have a child herself. What if there's sickle-cell anemia in the gene pool? Hmm? I'd certainly tell my kids."

"But tell them how, Norrie? Tell them that their grand-mother is a liar and apparently has been all her life? Thanks. That's a big help. The girls adore their Nana. I can't just dump this kind of shit on them."

"Inga is an adult," snapped Noreen.

"So? I'm an adult and it's rattled me."

"My, my, aren't you two testy," said Erin.

No one spoke to that comment. Claire trudged along, breathing with some difficulty as the path grew even steeper, while both Erin and Noreen took the climb as if an easy trot around the block. Lulu was clearly having a blast.

"Slow down, would you?" Claire said after a few more steps. "Jesus, we don't need to speed walk to the top, do we?"

"I'd say it's you who has slowed down," said Erin cheerfully. "Not used to these them hills anymore, flat-lander?"

"Very funny."

"I walk this trail almost every week," said Noreen virtu-ously, "to say hello to Harvey W. Scott, long ago editor of *The Oregonian* pointing his colossal bronze hand west. So the climb doesn't seem hard to me anymore. Remember our trip to Greece? Poor Claire, toiled up mild hills like they were the Alps. Or Golgotha."

"Excuse me, I have asthma?"

"I thought you said it was under control."

Claire shrugged. "I said mostly."

Just then, from over the rise, the dog yelped.

"Lulu!" Erin took off.

"Now what?" muttered Noreen, picking up the pace.

Claire felt the dog's cry slice right through her heart. She gasped, and tried to follow, but Noreen, too, vanished over the rise before Claire gained it and as she did, she could smell Lulu's problem: skunk. Her eyes watered, both from the stink and with relief it was nothing worse. The dog was whimpering but—

"She's okay," said Erin. "Except for the god-awful smell."

"Tomato juice," Claire offered weakly.

"Nah," said Erin. "She's done this little trick before. I have an emergency supply of skunk smell killer in the trunk. Hydrogen peroxide, baking soda, soap, and a bottle of dog shampoo."

"Which is why I can't stand dogs," said Noreen. "Wouldn't let the boys have one. Gah, how are you guys going to stand it, in the car?"

"We'll just have to stand it," said Erin.

"Phew!" Noreen pinched her nose closed.

"Better get back home. We can wash her on the driveway."

Claire nodded, happy to cut the hike short.

"Why don't you two come back over to my house tomorrow night?" asked Noreen. "Jim wants to say hello, and I'd like you to see my boys, maybe we can order a pizza or something."

"Sounds good," said Erin. "Come on you stinker, let's get off this hill."

"I haven't seen Jim in, what—" mused Claire.

"Twenty-one years," Noreen supplied, tight-lipped. "Just after Josh was born."

"So long," she murmured, her mind shuttling back to her father and that morning's time-warp conversation. "Where do the years go?" she said irritably.

"They really go!" said Erin. "Time keeps on ticking, ticking, ticking, into the future."

"Isn't that a line from a song or a poem?" asked Noreen, glancing over her shoulder at Claire. "Miss Literary Reference Book?"

"Yes," Claire replied. "Poem and song, both."

"Come on, Lulu, do not pull," said Erin. "We can't stay here, thanks to you."

"Well—my car's over there. See you guys tomorrow—say around 5:30? We can have a drink, then order. Phew!" Noreen crinkled her nose for emphasis and got into her semi-ancient, beat-up Datsun.

"I don't know a single other soul who doesn't adore a dog," whispered Erin to Claire as she unlocked the Civic.

"Sour-puss."

"Oh, come on, Nor was always dour—just a little less tart when she was younger. Anyway, I think she's got a bone to pick with both of us and doesn't even realize it." Erin pulled the Civic into little traffic on Burnside. "She stayed in Portland. We left." She glanced cautiously at Claire. "You, more or less permanently."

"What does that mean?"

Erin shrugged. "You haven't seen Jim in over twenty-*one* years. I bet she's got it calculated down to minute and second."

"And you have seen him, of course."

"When I visit my parents, I see Noreen and Jim. Always."

"Okay, true. The last time I saw Norrie was at your wedding—so email, phone calls, letters and cards aren't enough?" Claire hunched her shoulders. "I could pick a bone back. Only you've bothered to visit me Florida. Noreen hasn't."

"Is that fair? She can't afford to—Jim's on and off employed, and she can't raise her three boys on one lonely little librarian's salary. All I have to look after is myself, and Ms. Stinky-bum here."

"And your parents."

"Yeah, but I have well-heeled sisters."

"Norrie has a sister, doesn't she?"

"Some sister. I swear there isn't a recreational drug that woman won't try! I'm surprised she's still alive—you'd think her system would collapse. And lately—well, lately Rose has been suicidal. Right now, she's in rehab. The Currens are worried, of course, but they're both old and more ailing than my parents. He's deaf as a doornail and the Mrs. is on dialysis. Not a pretty picture."

"No, it isn't—not for any of us. Our parents' generation is dying." Claire sighed. "I knew Norrie's sister was a problem but not that big of a problem. Maybe I should be grateful, being an only child—" but those words, bringing back the whole mess of her parent's making, made her flinch. "I'm sorry, thinking of myself when I should be more concerned with Nor. It's just that I'm sort of quivering inside from it all, you know? Back there, when I heard Lulu cry, I nearly fainted."

"You are a wreck! What on earth did you think had happened?"

Claire shook her head. "I don't know. She fell off the hillside?"

"Only if the laws of gravity have been lifted. Gee, you are just a pit of gloom."

"Sorry. Can't help it."

"I know, I know. Listen, Claire, I'm just saying cut Noreen more slack. The two of you have been verbally pinching each other, and it's getting on my nerves." She pulled into the driveway. "Let's get this dog clean. Anyway, you need to give yourself some time to adjust, you know? You've been without a real father for most of your life, and you have your own life. Maybe it's time to just let it go?"

"Maybe. I don't know yet." Claire opened the door, but when she stood, she winced. "Uh-oh."

"Uh-oh what?"

"Damn, I think I hurt myself yesterday morning," she said, not wanting to return to the toxic place of her parents, although her words took her there anyway. "I mean physically. I rolled off the bed, and I think I might have ruptured this cyst on my back."

She lifted her t-shirt to touch the lump. "It feels hot."

"A cyst? You didn't tell you had a cyst."

"Of course not, silly, why would I? I didn't think about it! It's been there for years, and it isn't dangerous."

"If it's infected it could be dangerous."

"Yeah, I guess."

"You guess? You guess? I thought you were a doctor."

"I have a doctorate. Besides, I do mostly marine, not human biology." She huffed. "Maybe that's the problem, eh? Don't have enough human biology in my life."

"Whatever you say. My cell's in my purse—speed-dial 7, for the Portland free clinic. After we clean up stinky-girl here, we can stop by have it looked at."

Claire gazed out the window and murmured, "I feel like I need more than that."

"Come again?"

"I said *déjà vu*," she lied. "You're the one who took me to the clinic for that tetanus shot, remember? The day I punched a hole in my hand, in the garden?"

Erin nodded. "Yeah. What a fun day that was—the beginning of the end of The Red House."

Claire nodded, silent, remembering how she'd come home that day, laden with grocery sacks in both arms. She'd trudged up the concrete steps to the run-down Red House, and stood on the sagging front porch with a spaghetti squash casserole on her mind. She unlocked the massive, warped front door and toed it open with the blunt end of her Frye boot, when Erin called from inside, "I'm coming, let me help you!"

"What are you doing home?"

"I quit."

"You *what*?"

"Come on, let's get this stuff in the fridge."

"Okay—but the rest is still in the car." Handing off the two sacks, Claire stomped back down the steps to her red and cream VW bus, pockmarked and scratched but running like a Timex. Parked, it looked as if it were determined to climb up-hill by itself. She opened the side door, got the remaining two bags, shoved the squeaky door closed and went up the steep concrete steps again, and on inside to the kitchen.

"What do you mean, you quit?" she asked, setting the bags on the table, as Erin filled the vegetable bins of the fridge.

"Just what I said. Beets? Why beets? I hate beets."

"On sale." She glanced up at the clock. "Nor should be home by now."

"Yep. Fooling around with that guitar again but I think she's too lazy to ever be a rock star. More like a rock, period. Besides, she plays the piano better than that guitar."

"Don't tell her so."

"You think I'm nuts?" Erin backed up and closed the fridge. "She'd rip my head off. But I'm not holding my breath."

"At least she doesn't want to be a female Barry Manilow."

"Who in the hell would want—"

"My first college roommate. Linda. A doozy. Where'd you put the black beans?"

"Musta been a doozy all right. They're here." She handed Claire the can. "Mail came already—put yours in your room.

I'm going to get some writing in, before dinner. What are you making?"

Claire smiled and hefted a spaghetti squash. "Guess."

"Oh, no."

"Oh, yes. So why'd you quit?"

Erin shrugged. "I can't stand Brandon anymore. He's a lying-ass jerk."

"Okay, sure, but everybody knows he is—it's not a reason to quit."

"It is if you're me." Erin hung her head and frowned. Slowly, her face flushed a bright, blotchy red. "He's been hitting on me."

"Oh, no," said Claire. She put the squash on the counter, and gave her friend a rough hug, but Erin pushed her away, shaking her head. "I shouldn't be such a baby. And it's not my fault but I feel guilty anyway. Don't tell me I'm not. I know I'm not. Doesn't change the way I feel."

"What did he do?"

"Who?" asked Noreen, who'd come down to see what was for dinner.

"Brandon Barstow, the jerk," said Claire, glancing over to Noreen. "Erin's quit."

"You quit?"

Erin nodded. "Brandon's been hitting on me, and I just couldn't take it anymore. I told Dad about it—he's madder than a hornet, but what can I do? Don't say harassment, you know that's not going to work. You both saw how administration handled Susanne's complaint. So I'm quitting before I'm fired."

"Maybe we should all quit, then," said Noreen, nervously.

Erin eyed her friend. "And starve? Wait until I'm gainfully employed again, would you? Unless Brandon decides to hit on you, too."

"Oh, god—" said Noreen. "Can you imagine what Jim would do if that happened? He'd kill Brandon. Or at least try to."

"Speaking of starvation," said Claire, "I need to get dinner on. Do we have any parsley left in the garden?"

Noreen nodded, and Claire opened the screen door off the kitchen to the yard, where earlier that season the three of them had spent two days putting in various savory herbs, tomatoes, zucchini, pole beans, supplements to what they could afford from *Food Front*, the local co-op. She hurried down the rickety back steps, grabbed for the sheers they always left hanging on a hook against the house, and somehow missed. The pain made her shriek, which brought the other two running.

"What the hell—are you all right?"

"No," she said through clenched teeth. "I'm stuck—"

"Don't pull!" cried Noreen. "Wait and let me see—if you pull, you might hurt yourself worse." She bent her head close to the hook, and gingerly, with great care, disengaged Claire's palm, which began to run fast blood. "It's punctured," said Noreen, looking up at Erin. "Go get a towel or something, okay—Claire, listen to me. When was the last time you had a tetanus shot?"

Claire was staring at the welling blood covering her hand. "Does it look deep to you, Nor? Do you think I'll need stitches?"

"Maybe," said Noreen, folding her arms. "But you'll need a shot, if you haven't had one recently. It's a puncture wound— and that stupid hook is rusty. I knew it was a mistake, to leave it there. We could've kept the sheers in the junk drawer just as easily!"

Erin reappeared with a washcloth, which Noreen took and wrapped gently around Claire's hand as she said to Erin, "Why don't you take her down to the clinic—she's going to need a shot, at least. I'll make dinner."

"But it's my turn to cook," Claire said, with guilt.

"Well, you can't now, can you? You don't want lockjaw just to roast a spaghetti squash? Don't worry, silly-head. I promise I won't ruin your old casserole."

Seated in the waiting room at the downtown Portland Free Clinic, Claire felt the cyst on her back pulsing heat. But the waiting room was full, and they'd been told thirty minutes, at least. Erin flipped idly through one of the tattered magazines on a side table. Claire drummed her heels.

"I can't believe they still had my name on record," she said after awhile.

Erin looked up. "Lucky for you, though."

"This place doesn't look anything like the clinic I remember."

"No, they renovated a few years back. But the rest of downtown is pretty much the same. *Powell's* is still a landmark."

"And *Huber's,*" said Claire. "But the Northwest—phew you weren't kidding, it's so yuppified and upscale. I'm sorry they tore down The Red House."

"It was on the skids when we rented it."

"Too bad another *Rimsky Korsakoffee* couldn't have taken it on."

"I guess but no Louise Bryant ever lived in the Red House, and it wasn't haunted. Unless you count our dreams."

Claire turned to look full at her friend. "Do you feel you lost dreams there?"

Erin shrugged. "In a way. When we lived in The Red House, I felt every single day so intensely—like each moment was momentous, wholly life-altering. It's hard to believe we only had a year together. Felt like ten. And then we went our separate ways, and all that oomph, all that optimism and hope for the future that we shared, all those late, candle-lit pot-fueled gab sessions about love and life and all that jazz, poof! Gone."

"Well, sure, we were all twenty-something and full of ourselves."

"Best years of a life?"

Claire shook her head. "I'd love to have the energy of my twenty-odd old self. I'd love to have that body again—slender, responsive, without aches, or this dang cyst—I'd love, in a way, to have Inga be all of eight and still needing her Mom, but to have all that insecurity and struggle and sheer poverty? No. I may cook up a spaghetti squash for old times sake or because Ruth likes it, but to be unable to afford filet of sole or a lobster tail now and then? No thanks."

Erin sighed and threw the magazine she'd been leafing through back onto the scratched, beat-up waiting room table. "I know what you mean. Still sometimes I reach out—" she extended a fist and opened her hand like an anemone— "for her, for that girl I was, and like quicksilver—" she dropped her arm to her side— "she's gone."

"Mrs. Holt?" said a medical assistant. "This way please? Your friend can come with you, if you like."

"I'm coming," said Erin. "You know how stuff like this fascinates me."

Claire got up and reached for her purse. "Don't I? Honestly never understood why you didn't become a nurse."

Erin shrugged. "No head for chemistry."

They followed the assistant through a door to a corridor of doors, most of them shut, several with blinking red lights. The aide showed them both into one of these rooms, took Claire's blood pressure (too high!) and pulse (too fast!), gave her a paper gown and told her she could leave her jeans on, then left.

"Efficient," said Claire to the closed door. She started unbuttoning her shirt. "Of course my blood pressure and pulse are through the roof, whose wouldn't be? This won't be pleasant," she warned. "I've had it done once before and let me just say, the stuff that's inside a cyst is smelly."

"So what? We've already done skunk smelly today. Can't be worse than fresh skunk spray, can it?"

Claire wrinkled her nose in distaste. Cleaning the dog had been a chore. "Not that bad, I guess. Sebum smells and looks like old cheese."

"What kind? Limburger? Yum-yum."

"May I come in," said a voice, muffled by the door.

"Come on," replied Claire.

The P.A. who came in was a young blond woman, younger that the medical assistant had been. Wiry and almost nippy, she practically dashed into the room, reading from a chart. "Hi, my name's Hannah, and I'll be your surgeon for today."

"Surgeon?"

Hannah flashed a smile. "Joke. Says here you've got a sebaceous cyst, and that you think it's infected? If that's the case, I'll have to do an I&D."

"What a second," said Erin with mild alarm. "That sounds serious."

"Hardly," said Claire, her voice droll. "Incise and drain, correct?"

"That's about it," said Hannah. "Please turn over onto your tum-tum?"

Claire did as she was asked with reluctance. Laying flat on the examining table, her head turned to one side, she said, "How does it look?" She could feel Hannah's cool dry fingers palpating the lump.

"The good news is that I don't think it's infected. But you have ruptured the cyst wall, so it's best we go ahead and drain it. You'll feel a few little stings—that's me, injecting lidocaine with epinephrine around the cyst to numb it."

"Ouch."

"You okay?"

"She's okay," said Erin. "Just being a scaredy-cat."

"You know how much I love injections," muttered Claire, holding on to the sides of the examining table as if she might just melt off it.

"That's it. Now I am going to leave you two alone for a few minutes, to let the medication work. Are you comfortable enough on the table? Good. Do you want a magazine or anything?"

"No, thanks."

After Hannah had left, Erin remarked, "That's quite a lump you've got there."

"What does it look like?"

"A lump."

"Is it red? Does it look swollen?"

"Yes to both. Hey, Claire? I think we made the right decision. That thing looks angry. It's better you get rid of it."

Claire sighed, feeling over-exposed and trapped, caught up in *déjà vue* on the cold metal table. "Erin, you are always here for me, aren't you?"

"Come again?"

She tried to chuckle, but it sounded more like a whimper. "When I hurt myself, I mean. You always seem to be the one who takes care of me. When I punched a hole in my hand on the garden hook. Or when that bum, Drew, ran out on me—I was going to give Inga a father, what a mistake—and back to his wife, like a dog with his tail between his legs, leaving me holding the bag, as it were."

"That was bad."

"You're telling me? Herpes! And he denied it, too. Implied I'd slept around. What a shit. Why do I always fall for the shits, anyway?"

"I haven't exactly been lucky myself. Besides, David wasn't a shit."

"No," she agreed quietly. "But he wasn't around long, either. Only Noreen has stayed the long course of a marriage."

"And that hasn't been pretty. Here's your surgeon."

Hannah tore in as if on the tail of a tornado. "Ready?" she asked.

"As I'll ever be," muttered Claire.

"You might feel a little nick but if you feel pain, let me know."

"Righty-o."

Hannah put on a new pair of latex gloves, adjusted the light, and Claire felt a small pressure as an incision was made.

"Oh, nice," said Erin, watching. "What is that stuff called again?"

"Sebum," said Hannah, using a handful of sterile tissue to mop up the ooze. "I've smelled worse, although this cyst is pretty large."

"Hello? I'm still here, folks," said Claire. "What are you doing back there?"

"Squeezing," said Hannah. "I want to get this as empty as possible."

"I see what you mean, Claire. Cottage cheese and olive oil," said Erin.

"Yuck," muttered Claire. "Done yet?"

"Almost. I'm going to pack the empty cyst with gauze. Leave it in until Saturday. I'd advise you to have your own doctor take a look, just to be on the safe side. If he can, have him remove the cyst wall. Otherwise, it is likely to return. What he'll do is pull the cyst inside out, snip it off, and close with a couple stitches."

"How fun," said Claire drily.

"There," said Hannah. "I'm going to cover it for now, but after tonight, let it breathe. It'll heal faster. And I'm sending you off with some antibiotic cream. Keep it dry, cover it when you shower. You can sit up." She pulled off her gloves inside out and threw them in the trash.

Claire rolled over gingerly, gathering the paper robe into a semblance of dignity. The bandage pulled a little, but she was still numb from the lidocaine. "Do you—could I have some water?"

"Certainly," said Hannah. She took a Dixie cup from a dispenser, turned on the tap, washed her hands then filled the cup and handed it to Claire. Erin regarded her friend skeptically, her arms crossed over her chest.

"What?" said Claire. "Do I look frightening?"

Erin laughed. "You look like yourself on a bad hair day."

Claire stuck out her tongue.

Hannah sighed. "Well, I just leave you both now—I've got chin stitches to do on a bike accident. Kid's eight and screaming. Take care of your little wound and it shouldn't bother you."

"Will do, and thanks."

"No problem." With that, Hannah left.

"Get your clothes on, old girl," said Erin, "and let's get out of this here joint."

Claire slipped on her shirt. "Did you hear what she said? 'Your little wound' makes it sound almost sweet. Ah, my little wound, come to your Mama. The bandage feels funny."

"Never mind the bandage, how do you feel?"

"Light-headed. A little woozy." Claire made a wry face. "Too much excitement crammed into too few days for the old girl, I guess."

"I expect food will help."

Claire nodded, stood and steadied herself. She picked up her purse, took a few steps and said. "Okay. I'm ambulatory."

"I should hope. Not like you had brain surgery or anything."

"Careful," said Claire, giving Erin a comic glare. "My little wound might hear you belittling her, and get all enflamed again."

The Brennan's house in Southeast Portland in the Mt. Tabor neighborhood was the same one the couple had rented as newlyweds. Chocolate brown shingles with a grey, mottled roof and a front porch a little too much at the perpendicular, built in the 'fifties or late forties, the house had, to Claire's eye, the tattered look of something well-loved, a look she fancied her father's home had wholly lacked. This house sat high up off the sidewalk on a hillock, braced by a concrete wall into which stairs had been cut, and looked a little precarious, as if it were leaning, ever so slightly, over the pedestrians below. Shaded by two handsome maples, the porch boasted a swing on which one of the boys had left a baseball glove.

Claire regarded the place thoughtfully. The last time she'd been inside was just after Joshua Brennan had been born and just before she left the West Coast for Boston to finish her graduate studies. She'd been twenty-nine. The house hadn't really changed, not on the outside.

You have, though she thought. *We all have. So damned much.*

This came to her even more forcefully when Erin and she, having been met by Noreen at the screen door, were led through both living room and kitchen into the TV room. Jim Brennan was stretched out on the same couch he'd been lying upon when Claire had last seen him, as a haggard new father, tired and proud. He rose from the couch to greet them, almost exactly as he had done years ago, and once again not thrilled to be dragged away from one endless baseball game after another on the television. Claire felt all the years that had folded up on her and vanished that first day in the Civic with Erin now unfold like an accordion pleat, aggressively reasserting the stony reality of time. Jim's beard, once red, was multi-colored, reddish, brown, grey, and white and his hairline was no more, it had receded until his forehead dove behind the rise of his head.

"Claire, what a pleasure," she heard him say, but it came out garbled, as if he wore dentures, and without a shred of enthusiasm

"Jim," she said evenly. "How are you?" *God this is awkward,* she thought.

He nodded and sat back down on his couch, which had to belong to him and him alone, as Claire couldn't imagine any other living being that would dare sit on that thing.

"Erin," he said. "How's the Bay Area doing you?"

"Fine as usual, Jim. Listen, we don't want to interrupt the game—Nor, why don't we go see about ordering some pizza?"

"I don't like anchovies," said Jim, glued to the small TV screen.

Noreen rolled her eyes dramatically. "I know." She turned on her heel, with Erin and Claire at it. Back in the kitchen, she went to the back door and called to her sons, Calvin and Matt, who were passing a football back and forth in the yard.

"I'm going to order pizza—any special requests?"

Claire clasped her hands behind her back, and tried not to notice the teetering pile of dirty dishes in the double sink; or the several corners where the linoleum curled away from the floor; or the alarmingly indeterminate smudges on the faded wallpaper. Erin, clearly more at home than Claire could feel, was rummaging in a junk drawer to find the local pizza parlor's menu, as she murmured, "I think they have artichokes on one of their specials, don't they Nor?"

Noreen turned. "The boys want onions and Italian sausage."

"Don't they have an artichoke—"

"Oh, yes," Noreen peered into the junk drawer, pushed aside a pair of scissors and a ball of twine to extract a limp, well-used menu. "Artichoke and shrimp, with red peppers and broccoli—my favorite, though I don't get to have it often. Josh calls shrimp the insects of the sea. Won't touch one. But since you're here—" she grinned and put the menu down on a counter— "I'm ordering two for the three of us!" She opened the fridge. "White wine, or red?"

"White for me," said Erin, reaching into cupboard and taking out three plastic glasses, then hesitated. "Will Jim want some?"

"Beer," said Noreen as she handed Erin a bottle of Chardonnay. "He thinks wine is for women only, or for men with limp wrists—his description, not mine. Claire? Red or white?"

"White. Hey, Nor? Can I use the bathroom?"

"No," said Noreen seriously, then she smiled. "Of course, silly, you remember where it is, surely?"

"Top of the stairs."

"See you in a pinch."

The shared bathroom in the house—as opposed to the one off the master, ground-floor bedroom—was at the top of a steep staircase that took a right angle turn at the first landing, underneath a window—the second floor had once been no more than an attic, but after Calvin's birth, Jim had refinished the attic to accommodate the boys. Climbing those stairs gave Claire the uneasy sensation that at any moment she'd be propelled back down them, tush first; she also tried hard to ignore the fact that if Erin's house-keeping skills were iffy at best, Noreen had just given up. Mincing around the cramped bathroom, she decided to air-dry her hands. On the way back down, she paused at the window to watch the boys horsing around out back—two big boys, they had Noreen and Jim's height, both of them; Calvin was a redhead, Matthew a blond. Joshua, away at college, was the dark one. Watching them made Claire's heart droop; she not seen them in so long, they were strangers to her and the years that had so aggressively reasserted themselves earlier now elongated, stretching like un-familiar miles before her, with no sign or roadmap as to how to navigate them. She leaned against the windowsill and closed her eyes, seeing Ruth's face in the dark. Noreen had never seen Ruth, except in holiday photographs. She and Jim had never even met David and now, they never would.

"Claire? Have you gotten lost or something?" That was Erin. "Your wine is sweating bullets, waiting on you."

"Coming!"

When the last piece of shrimp and artichoke pizza lay wilted and cold in the delivery box and the Three Musketeers had killed not one but two bottles of Chardonnay, they had devolved back into the giggling twenty-somethings they knew each other to be, at heart, cracking old jokes. Noreen's two boys had excused themselves early, clearly as ill at ease with Claire as she felt with them, and Jim had taken a last beer back to the TV. So, a bit tipsy, the three women strolled down the block and up two others, to a short row of shops, one of which served as a deli-coffee-dessert cafe.

"Just a regular, with a shot of vanilla," said Claire, the last of the three to order.

"Wuss," said Erin. "How about a caramel crème latte with a shot of espresso?"

"What and stay up all night with the jitters?"

Noreen had seated herself in a booth with an Earl Grey and a chocolate chip cookie. As Claire paid for her coffee, Erin took her latte over to the table. Stashing away her change, Claire took a few moments to look at her two old friends, surreptitiously, in a mirror. Erin was saying something that looked urgent, Noreen had her eyes shut, and Claire thought *they are wearing me out. This whole trip is wearing me out.* She picked up her coffee, feeling the bandage on her back pull a little. It pulled again when she sat down.

"I was just saying to Nor, she and I should come to Florida, just the two of us. The boys can take care of themselves for a week, surely?"

Noreen shook her head. "Maybe. I'm not sure."

"You know you two are welcome, anytime," said Claire.

Erin did a double take. "Say again?"

"You're welcome, anytime. I'd love to have you."

"Don't lie, Claire," said Noreen wearily.

"What?" Claire was appalled. "I'm not lying."

Erin sipped her coffee. "Let's just say that's about the most tepid invite I've heard in recent memory. Rote."

Claire shook her head. "I'm sorry if it sounded insincere. I'm tired. I shouldn't have had all that wine and I've got a hole in my back."

"Oh come off it," said Noreen. "A hole in your back! You have a teensy little incision for a harmless little cyst. Not like that mother of a boil I had to have lanced last year—you saw it, Erin. Now that was ugly—and how Biblical? I mean, a boil. Sinners and saints endure boils. Isn't it one of the plagues Moses calls down on the Egyptians?" She held up her hand. "There were ten." She began to count them off finger by finger. "Blood, frogs, gnats, flies, boils—"

"Do we have to go through a Sunday school lesson?" said Erin irritably.

Noreen placed her hand down on the table. "I teach Sunday school."

"I know you do," said Erin. "You know I know you do."

Silence.

Claire, feeling as if Noreen had poked her with two fingers in the eyes, stared down into her coffee mug, willing herself into sobriety. *Am I insincere? Perhaps—I had just been wishing myself home.* Mercifully, her cell phone rang, and she excused herself to answer it, stepping outside the coffee shop.

"Hi Mom!"

"Ruth! Oh, sweetheart, it's good to hear your voice."

"I'm sorry to call so late—"

"—it's not that late—"

"—but I just had to talk to you! Mom, guess what! Coach says I'm finally good enough to make a run for the Olympics, in 2008. I can't believe it!"

Stunned, Claire leaned against a window front. All she could think to say was, "You'll be eighteen."

"So? I don't care if I'm a little older than everybody else. I have to give it a shot. I have to. It'll mean extra training, loads more discipline, but I can handle it. Don't you think I can handle it?"

"Of course you can I'm just—surprised. I didn't know it was something you wanted. Or were even thinking about."

"I told Inga, but I didn't want to talk to you about it if it couldn't ever happen, I mean, Mom, how embarrassing! But Coach finally gave me the green light, and he's found me a real Olympic coach already. I've got to try."

"It's marvelous, of course, a marvelous chance, Ruth, my goodness—are you sure—I mean—I'm—but Inga has always said you cut the water like a knife."

"Oh, Inga is awesome, Mom. She's been my best friend in all this, really, encouraging me to swap gymnastics for the diving board and all."

Claire held her breath for a moment. "I'm so glad and you know I'll help you, too. In any way I can."

"Oh, I know, Mom. It's just—well, I didn't want to disappoint you and basically I just can't disappoint my big sister. All she wants is for me to do what I want to do."

"But Ruthie, that's all I've ever wanted for you! To be happy."

"Sure, sure, I know, but I can't be happy if I make you sad, can I? But that's all over, now that I've got Coach on my side. I'm going to work like I've never done before. I want to medal—for you. For Dad."

Claire's eyes stung. "Your father would be so proud of you, Ruth."

"Yeah."

"I miss him. Everyday," she murmured.

"Yeah," Ruth breathed and let the silence hang.

Does she still blame me a little? thought Claire. *For indulging his love of flight?*

Then, "Mom? I gotta go. Max and Inga and me are going out to celebrate a little. See you Sunday."

Claire snapped her cell phone closed, and stared at it for a few moments wondering how it was possible she could have missed any sign of her daughter's Olympic ambition, and muttered to herself, "shit," as she realized that Inga had been hinting around about it for some time.

"What is wrong with you, Claire Holt?" she murmured aloud, now wanting more than anything to be home, in her home, in beautiful, tropical Florida, with her daughters and the future—not stuck miles away in chilly Oregon, floundering in the past. She came up for air, slipped the phone in her pocket and went back to face her friends.

Later, she'd remember that evening as the worst of her trip because when she stepped back inside the coffee shop, Noreen was weeping, sobbing really, as Erin sat frozen in her seat, a look of blank astonishment on her face.

"No," she was saying, as Claire hurried over and asked, "What's wrong?"

Erin shook her head as Noreen, glared up through tears at the two of them. "Josh wants to be a Marine, and Jim supports him. Two against one."

Claire sat down. "Joshua? No."

"Yes," said Noreen. She grabbed her napkin and roughly wiped her cheeks. "He's a bright kid, my kid and he's going to throw his life away, to impress his unhappy father. Or something like that. I can't imagine where he got the idea to join the Marines. It could not have been from me."

"I've heard they've got a lot of recruiters on campuses these days," said Claire lamely, not knowing what else to say.

Noreen pursed her lips and shook her head. Her eyes had a fuzzy, far away look in them, and she squeezed the napkin into a tiny ball. "He'll be sent to Afghanistan. Or Iraq or whatever hell we've decided to meddle with, and then come back in pieces. Or in a body bag."

"Nor," said Erin sharply. "Stop it."

Noreen tried to focus. She sighed. "I need to go home, girls. Now. Take me home, would you? Say goodnight and take the old lady home."

Erin stood up and gave Noreen her arm; Claire followed, her mood sinking out of sight, especially as they all hugged and said goodbye because she and Erin had to leave in a day, and Noreen had to work. Driving back across the dark

Willamette River, and past the glittering downtown for the umpteenth time in one week, neither Claire nor Erin spoke—it seemed to Claire she'd used up her entire reserve of emotional fuel, and would have to run on fumes, all the way back to Florida.

Chapter Four

Wintering

As the plane lifted up over the Bay, making a wide curve to head East, Claire sat alone, miraculously alone in her row, so she shifted over to the window-seat and gazed down at the shoreline, trying to imagine the Farallon Islands, out beyond the Golden Gate. The restaurant of the same name, *Farallon*, in Union Square, where Erin had taken her for a send-off supper, had been a pleasant whimsy of a place, and the food, "coastal cuisine" had been beyond excellent, but the floating jelly-fish pendant lamps and the odd little wall mosaic she'd faced during dinner, of a man in an old-fashioned diving bell helmet, 1920's bathing suit and sneakers on the sea floor being served a martini while he made a sketch of a rubber duck perched next to a fat red starfish made the scientist in her curious about the flora and fauna of those tiny, exposed islands and even more curious about the Gulf of Farallones, with its complex of marine life. She knew a little bit about the Gulf because one of the people she'd contacted as she groped her way to a new grant proposal was working on sea stars there, but she'd never visited herself.

She tapped the Plexiglas of the plane's window thoughtfully. Perhaps she would have to return to the West Coast after all. Maybe. Maybe not.

Claire closed her eyes and sighed. It was too soon to contemplate another visit. She wanted to be home—she needed to see a palm tree, so she thought instead about how she'd spent yesterday afternoon, to avoid thinking about anything more serious. While Erin finished up some minor editing at the office before they were to head off to the *Farallon* farewell dinner, Claire found herself almost mindlessly returning to Petfinder. com, numbly peering at one abandoned and humanless pup after another, all seeking a good, loving permanent home. Each furred face made her wonder about their ultimate fates, which in turn had made her morose about the brevity of every goddamn thing under the sun, including the sun—*Bud and I had twelve good years,* she thought. *He was more constant than anyone but my girls, and far less of a worry. The girls can get hurt. Still can. Bud forgot his hurts in a mere second. Memory, but no memories, everything present tense—like Mom can be sometimes, now. How blessed is that?*

She clasped her hands hard, knowing her mother's condition was anything but blessed, really. She had good days, bad days. Wasn't living, that. Surviving.

"May I get you something to drink?" said the steward, breaking into her thoughts. She looked up, and tried to make her face neutral, cheerful even.

"Coffee, please. Black."

But as she sipped her drink, her unfinished and by now stuck-in-the-mud grant proposal rose up before her like a sea monster, and she turned her back on it, too, only to have her graduate class, the new one she'd been designing, take its place. The fall semester was three months off, but it was already crowding her, all because of the damn grant proposal that she had so hoped to finish, before her sabbatical ran out, and hadn't.

"Too much," she murmured. "Too much." She shook her head, opened the tray in front of her. When she'd first sat down, she'd taken her black moleskin notebook out of her bag; now she picked it up and opened it again, to the Adelaide Crapsey poem on the flyleaf. During the visit she'd not managed even a moment to add anything else, she'd been so busy. Her mind went as blank as the page she gazed at. She retrieved a pen from her pocket, and, after a moment's hesitation wrote—

This past week has been like some kind of emotional endurance experiment. Why does life come at one in hard indigestible lumps? Bud, that was one awful thing, but he'd had a good life. Finding my so-called father again—my black father? Black. God, what would Jordan's family say to that little bombshell? This is all quite another thing, all of it. How could anyone, anyone for any reason, just walk out on a child? I know people do it. I know I sound like an idiot, unfamiliar with the horrors of the daily news—father beats child to death, mother drowns five children—and yet still I ask: how could he do that to me? All right, he told me why. He had reasons. Selfish reasons. And Mom—what about Mom's lie?"

Claire lifted the pen off the page. She'd poked the tip through the paper, she was that upset. Carefully, she laid the pen down for a moment, to take a deep breath, thinking maybe it was time to take another meditation or yoga class because *you will never solve the past, you are fifty, get over it*—when the seatbelt sign went on, the plane dipped a bit, her stomach flipped over and the pilot's calm voice said, "Folks I've been told we're in for some rough air. Nothing to worry about, but

I ask you—and the cabin attendants—to please take your seats, and fasten your seat-belts, until further notice."

Claire grabbed her pen before it rolled away, clutched her notebook shut and endured another gut-wrenching drop. Just behind her headrest, a passenger somewhere gasped and all she could think of was David, she could see him as clearly as if he were sitting next to her, his craggy, studious face marked by early acne scars that he hid behind a full beard, his dark curly hair just beginning to show threads of silver, those brown eyes as soft and sweet as a boy's. It was his dream to own that Navaho Piper—a dream she helped him achieve, by saving out some money across a year. But he'd gotten to enjoy his plane for less than a year—the last time she'd flown with him, they'd gone from St. Augustine all the way up to the Vineyard, both to celebrate their anniversary and so that she could give a lecture at the Woods Hole Oceanographic Center.

The plane dropped again; Claire ground her teeth and closed her eyes.

"Don't you trust me?" he'd shouted at her over the sputter of the Piper's engine, on the morning they'd taken off for the Vineyard. "I've been a pilot longer than we've been married, Claire!"

"I know," she'd said through her nerves as she buckled in. "Air is not my element. Air is murderous!"

"Come again?"

She raised her voice. "Air is not my element, I would rather breath water!"

He grinned. "Yeah, I know. You're a mermaid."

She shrugged. "Ruth's the mermaid! But water is my element, not air"

He laughed. "You can't even swim the breaststroke!"

"Details! I dog paddle. I manage."

He shook his head and taxied out toward the runway as she watched the ground start slipping by. Once aloft, the engine didn't seem quite as loud and the craft didn't seem quite as flimsy and the sky had been clear as a bell, clear up the coast to New England, only one small patch of turbulence to mar the gorgeous day that marked their ninth, and last anniversary—because the air did prove murderous and David never made it to their tenth.

The plane shuddered and slowly smoothed out, but the seatbelt sign stayed on and the cabin crew stayed put. Claire opened her journal again and smoothed out the page she'd crumbled by mistake. She read what she'd written, and then added a command for herself: Ask Mom. But as she put away the journal in favor of a Ross MacDonald novel she'd picked up in the SFO airport, she knew scripting that particular command—*Ask Mom*—was easier by far than it would be to carry out.

Jane Holt sat in her wheelchair beside the white baby grand piano in one of the common rooms, her gaze resolutely fixed on the keys. Her nurse had dressed her to the nines for Mass, her white hair pinned neatly up under an old piece of lace. Despite her humped back and gnarled hands, Jane Holt maintained a certain air, a superiority that bordered on the smug, a woman used to being obeyed, and Claire had almost always obeyed her—almost. Her teenage passion for Jordan Valery had been her first, costly rebellion, while marrying David Rothstein— "a Jew this time? Can't you find a nice white boy?" her mother had muttered—the last, but the most enduring rebellion had been her intense love of science. It was something Jane just couldn't grasp, and never wanted to understand.

"It isn't womanly," she had often complained when Claire had eagerly brought home yet another science project. "Smelly formaldehyde and messy dissections are for boys, not a young lady like you."

Still, thought Claire, *Mother never stood in my way. Never tried to make me into someone I wasn't—except in one way I never knew, until now.*

"Ma?" she said gently. "Did you hear me?"

"Of course I heard you, I'm not deaf."

"Well? Isn't the sweater you're wearing the one you thought your day-nurse had stolen? Poor Takesha puts up with a lot."

Jane gave her daughter a look the family had nicknamed The Glare. She pulled herself up in the wheelchair and said, archly, "This sweater isn't yellow. This sweater is maize."

"Maize?" Claire burst out laughing. "If you say so, Mother."

Jane shifted her weight a little, without taking her eyes off the piano. "Once upon a time, I could play that thing."

"Yes, Mother. But—"

"Where are the girls?"

"I just told you," Claire said impatiently, and glanced up at a utilitarian plastic clock on the wall above the reception desk. "They'll be here to take us for lunch, but that's not for a half hour. I need to know—"

"You were always needing to know, weren't you, Claire? How does a frog tick? Where do tadpoles come from?" Suddenly she wheeled around and gave her daughter the once over. "Still cutting live starfish up into little bits, at your age!"

Claire laughed. "At my age? Mom, I'm a marine biologist. It's my job."

"Some job. Still in school, holed up in some dank little lab. When are you going to retire and enjoy yourself?"

"I do enjoy myself. But I don't want to talk about me, I want to talk—"

"—about your father, that man!" Jane stared at her daughter for a moment. "I can't believe you went and found him out."

"Ma, I—"

"Meddling."

"But Ma—"

"I should have listened to my own grandmother, and left him well enough alone! You know what she said to me, at that Christmas party where I met him? She said, 'Look at that boy, Jane. You see what he just done? He went and took himself the nicest cut of meat. That's a selfish boy, Jane, a spoiled boy, I'm warning you.' She was right, but did I listen to her? No. I thought: she's an idiot, always bowing to other people, church folk, white people, stuck cleaning out bed-pans, doling out pills." Jane huffed. "Your Father would have ruined your life for you, Claire. You're old enough to remember how much of a chance any colored child had, back in those days! How far along in your science classes would you have gotten? Besides, look at me—look at you! We're not Negro. Good hair, light skin, that's what even my own grandmother used to say, I'm more white than anything else, Negro was just bad luck on a birth certificate. Why not make use of what I actually had, get the hell out of the South? Your Father went for it, at first. He passed. Can't say he was unhappy as a white man, either, not until all the other troubles started."

"Troubles? Do you mean the Civil Rights Movement?"

"I mean troubles, all the troubles! Vietnam took one good boy after another, Vatican II ruined the Church, girls in blue jeans running loose like whores, doing drugs, boys with hair like I never seen before, people marching for this thing and that thing—trouble, and I wanted no part of it. I wanted a quiet and safe life, for myself and for you, and I knew how to get it, too. Your father obviously didn't."

"Things have changed," said Claire. "We don't live in that world anymore."

"Maybe you don't and maybe, just maybe, my grandchildren don't but I really wouldn't know and if you dare, *dare* tell anyone here in this hellish place that I am not as white as I look, I will never speak to you again."

"Mother! Is that a nice thing to say?"

"No, but I'm not a nice person and never have been. Nice is a word for the witless, and I don't have the patience for witless people. If you were frank with yourself, neither do you, you've never been one to put up with idiots. Makes you a tough teacher, I've no doubt."

Claire glanced away. "I am a tough teacher."

"Of course you are. You were always very intense. It scares the nice ones away."

"The witless ones, you mean."

Jane shrugged, insofar as she still could.

"Well," said Claire. "What shall I do about Dad?"

"That man can go to hell for all I care."

"Fine," said Claire meditatively. "But what should I tell the girls about it all?"

Jane glanced up, and her defiant eyes also held fear. "Nothing," she whispered. "Don't, Claire. Don't say anything. Not about me. I don't care what you tell them about that man, you tell them what you like, but not about me."

"Did you ever love him, Mom?"

Jane's face stiffened, and the corners of her lips grew pale. "Loved him? How can you ask that, how can you, Claire? Wicked girl."

"Mom, please," said Claire, with a *frisson* of anger.

Jane closed her eyes. "Loved him? I didn't just love him. I adored him. He became my world, when we left Alabama. I left everything I'd ever known and he became all I had, until—" she stopped. "You tell the girls what you like, but not about me. Never about me."

"But it affects them, doesn't it? They have a right to know who they are, where they came from, don't they?"

Jane's mouth trembled, and she closed her eyes on a tear. Claire sat down, taking one of her mother's deformed and slightly shaking hands gently in her own. "Never mind, Mom. What's done is done. Don't worry. I won't tell your two Dolly Dimples. It'll be between you and me."

"Promise?"

"I promise," Claire lied. "They should be here, any minute." She glanced down at her now-tiny mother and said, "Will you promise me something?"

"What?"

"Lay off Max."

"Max? Come on, now, Max knows I'm just kidding."

"Mom."

"You don't mean to say he's been taking my jokes seriously? So maybe I was hard on him, at first, but—"

"It bothers Inga."

"Oh, please, that girl has no sense of humor. Serious as a clock," Jane said and slowly pulled a tissue out of her sleeve, to dab at her damp cheek. "Where are we going for lunch?"

"I told you already, *Salt Water Cowboys.*"

Jane broke into a broad smile. "My favorite!"

"Of course. And both Inga and Ruth have news for you. Good news."

"Oh?" said Jane with caution. "Will I think it is good news?"

Claire smiled. "That's why I'm telling you, now, please, Mother, to hear what they have to say as good news? Agreed?"

"Oh dear," murmured Jane. "Yes, dear."

"There they are," Claire said, stationing herself behind the wheelchair, and taking hold of the handles as Max held open the door for his wife and sister-in-law. A thin, spry figure of a man, Max was a long-distance marathon runner, when he wasn't teaching Shakespeare to expensive undergraduates in an exclusive Northern college. Taller than both her husband and her younger sister, Inga nearly pushed Ruth inside with quick, awkward glance backwards. Spying her mother and Nana, she smiled and said, "It is going to pour, any minute now."

"Come give your Nana a kiss, Ruthie," said Jane in that peculiar, singsong voice she used on all children, even grown ones. "How is my Dolly Dimples?"

"I'm good," she said, kissing Jane lightly on her cheek. She gave her mother a questioning look, and Claire shook her head slightly thinking once again how strongly Ruth took after her father—*what had happened to my side of the gene pool? Except for her skin and the oval shape of her face, Ruth is all Rothstein.*

"How do you feel today, Nana?" asked Inga.

Jane looked up. "The same. I wish I could get out of this chair."

"I know," said Ruth. "Here, Mom, let me push," and she nudged Claire aside with her elbow, took hold of the wheel-chair's handles and started wheeling her grandmother toward the door, whispering something that made Jane titter.

"How'd your little chat go?" asked Inga.

Claire shook her head. "She's dead set against you and Ruth knowing."

"That figures," said Max. "You didn't really expect—"

"No," Claire admitted, trying to keep the bitter taste in her mouth from saturating her next words. "She has always gotten her way, and it's far too late to change things now. I just wish—" she stopped and bit her lower lip.

"If wishes were horses, beggars would ride. Isn't that what you've always said?"

Claire turned a half-amused, half-troubled glance on her daughter. "Another old chestnut of your Nana's, sweetheart. But I'm sure I've said it since I know them all by heart, now. A stitch in time saves nine. A bird in the hand is worth two in the bush. Here's your hat, what's your hurry?" she choked up a little on the last one, thinking about her father, how he used to leave the house in the morning all in a rush for work, grabbing his respectable, 1950's fedora off the coat rack and jamming it on his head, as if he couldn't get away fast enough.

Their short trip from the assisted living facility over to *Salt Water Cowboy's*, a unique and very old watering hole in St. Augustine Beach, was for the most part silent and, for Claire, tense. She sat beside her mother in the back seat, with Ruth on the other side while Max drove and Inga kept him company in the front. Claire knew her mother thought Max drove recklessly, even at a crawl; Inga knew it, too, and looked green with worry that Nana would say something cutting or mean. Ruth sat staring out the window, unusually silent, and Claire couldn't think of a safe thing to say, unless she wanted to be inane, and talk about gas prices or the weather—which she didn't want to do.

Finally, it was Jane herself who broke the tension. "Ruthie? Inga? Your mother tells me you both have good news? Well? Let's have it!"

Inga turned full around and stammered, "I—I was waiting until we were seated."

Ruth took one look at her sister's face and said, "I'll go first, then, Nana. Besides, I think Inga's news is way better than mine, and worth champagne—don't you, Mom?"

"Absolutely," said Claire heartily. "But don't sell yourself short, Ruth."

"Well?" said Jane, impatiently. "How long are you going to keep your old Nana in the dark? Let at least one cat out of the bag, please?"

Ruth took her grandmother's hand in both of her own. "I'm going to try out for the 2008 summer Olympic diving team, Nana. What do you think of that?"

Jane blinked a few times before she said, "Oh, Ruthie, that's—I—that's breath-taking!"

Ruth laughed, "Don't get me on the team before I've qualified. But I'm like going to try, real hard!"

"You'll make it," said Jane firmly.

"I hope so, I mean, like I sure need the confidence, Nana. I just hope I can keep, like, feeling it." Ruth shivered a little. "I mean—well! Everybody knows what I mean."

"And here we are," said Max as he let the car roll into a space on the dusty, unpaved end of Dondanville Road, a residential street that dead-ended at a salt marsh, on which, or over which, *Salt Water Cowboys* had been built, an old-fashioned, cracker-style house, looking more like an overgrown, tin-roofed shack. Max leaned over the front seat and said, "I'll get the wheelchair—why don't you get us a table, huh, Claire?"

"I'll help you," said Ruth to Max.

Inga said, "I'll go with Mom."

Jane folded her hands in her lap and said, "All settled then."

Claire slipped her arm in Inga's as they walked across the white chalk parking lot to the wooden ramp of the restaurant, which jutted out into the marsh on stilts. "You shouldn't be nervous, sweetheart," she said. "Nana's not going to bite. She's got a searing sense of humor, I'll grant but—"

Inga laughed nervously. "She does, though. Bite."

"Only because you are closer to a daughter to her than Ruth is—more like me, and you know how she takes her pot-shots at me."

Inga rolled her eyes. "Don't I."

"Goodness, the marsh smells tonight," said Claire, gazing down at one of the restaurant's resident ginger cats—she'd once heard a waiter guesstimate the pack totaled fifty, most of them some version of ginger, with a few stray grays and blacks, some with long, elegant tails, others with knob ends, a genetic defect similar to Hemingway's six-toed cat's descendants in Key West.

Inga pulled open the door, nodding her mother inside. "Age before beauty," she said, to which Claire replied, "Ha!"

A young, sun-blond man asked them "a table for how many?"

"Five."

"Table for five—follow me," and he grabbed a handful of plastic menus.

Claire wrinkled her nose. *Salt Water Cowboys* was always redolent with both frying oil and mold, and no amount of bleach or ammonia could quite cover the combination. The young man led them to a round table smack in the middle of the largest room, from which they could see the marsh out the windows all about them. Claire sat down in the rustic, rather rickety wooden chair, as Inga planted herself next to her mother and said,

"I think Nana is going to throw a fit. I just know it."

"If she does, she'll hear from me. You will make yourself positively sick worrying about her reaction. Who knows, maybe she'll surprise you."

Inga picked up a menu, sighing.

When Ruth and Max wheeled Jane to the table, she said, impatiently, "Inga why on earth are you looking at the menu? You must know it by heart, by now, and besides you always have the same thing as I do—"

"—but they have specials, Nana—"

"—fried shrimp."

"I've been a little off fried things lately," murmured Inga as Max sat down next to her. Under the table, he took his wife's hand and squeezed it.

"Did you just say you've been a little off fried things?"

"Yes, Nana. Fried food hasn't been agreeing with me."

"What? You never ate anything but fried shrimp when you were little. You must be sick. Are you sick?"

Inga shook her head.

Claire said, "Let's order that champagne, shall we?"

"Max and Inga are going to have a baby!" blurted Ruth, unable to stand the tension any longer and unwilling to see her sister suffer. "Isn't that wonderful, Nana? I'm going to be an auntie. Auntie Ruthie."

Inga's eyes welled up and spilt. She wiped at them and laughed. "Sorry. My hormones are out of whack. So, Nana, what do you think?"

Jane cocked her head, and looked back and forth at her two granddaughters, but said nothing, just pursed her lips.

Claire crossed her arms. "Mother?" she prompted.

"Well, I never," said Jane meditatively. "I never did expect to live long enough to be a Great-Granny. Ah, me—will wonders never cease! Max? Inga? Come and give your old Nana a kiss." And just like that, the unpromising lunch grew warm. Jane still had that kind of power, and knew it, and so, Cheshire-like, she smiled serenely over her familial domain, as the afternoon waned into evening.

Driving across the temporary bridge built to sustain St. Augustine traffic while the famous—or infamous—*Bridge of Lions* was repaired, Claire squinted into the low sunlight, past the jam of masts in the harbor to the strip of A1A on the other side, musing idly that it was going to take a long, long time to finish the bridge repair, far longer than any estimate she'd ever heard. Having spent the day doing some early Christmas shopping, both in town and at the outlet mall, she was a bit disappointed, having hoped but failing to get a jump on the season, which always seemed to rush down on her as if a seasonal freight train.

"The fall semester is always the 100-meter dash," she murmured to herself as she switched lanes, glad to be part of the Whitney and not on the main campus, not this fall. From all she heard, the University of Florida's Administration in Gainesville had lost it's collective mind, deep-sixing the humanities, de-funding crucial research, trying as one colleague said, to make UF into Florida Tech, all of which added weight to the blue-black stone of anxiety she was still carting around with her, a bit smaller since she'd found her father, *no matter how painful it is*, she thought, *knowing him seems better than not.*

Yet still she felt the weight of whatever it was, tucked into a pocket of her heart, solid, like a worry-stone. One of the few thoughts that lightened the worry was that the Whitney, mercifully, had been spared so far—*yes, only because we're perpetually in the hole, always begging for scraps as Gloria used to say* she thought, eager to get to the lab for an hour or so before she had to go home and start dinner. Ruth wouldn't be back from practice until after seven, and she found herself sharply missing Inga, yet again. Five months had passed already since her eldest had gone home from vacation; five whole months since Claire's trip to San Francisco, too, a stretch of summer that had birthed yet another national tragedy, Hurricane Katrina. She and Ruth had watched the Weather Channel obsessively, as they had done every summer since Andrew struck Miami. *The hurricane season just seems to grow longer and stronger*, she thought. They had watched Katrina, though, in a kind of fascinated Floridian horror, half composed of guilty relief that this one, this giant, wasn't headed their way at least—the 2004 season had cross-stitched the state with devastation. So they'd followed the red, spinning hurricane symbol named Katrina churn up the Gulf, gaining the muscle it would use to flatten New Orleans, as if General William Tecumseh Sherman had risen from the dead to become the sea; once again, a grand, gracious southern city, yet also terrible in its particular form and shape of brutality, smote to ruin.

Five months: a busy, sometimes scary, but certainly out-right angering summer—an anger that welled whenever she flashed upon all those people, most poor, mostly black, abandoned in the swamp that had once been New Orleans. She didn't really know anyone there; she'd only visited once, on vacation with Nana and Ruth, before Jane had become too crippled to travel. Jane, of course, denied any connection to the city, even if she was proud of something she would never not call Creole in her past. Claire had wondered, briefly, about it at the time, and wondered more now but Jane was bent on taking that tidbit of the family past with her to the beyond. Meanwhile, there was the horror show of Katrina and the whole thing reeked of a willed impotence on the part of the government, and even if she'd donated clothes and food and money, anything she could think of, to help, it didn't help with the rage.

But she was caught up in another kind of impotence, too—or passive resistance because although she should have or could have contacted either Erin or Noreen, just to keep in touch, check-in, see how they were, for some reason, she couldn't make herself do it, make herself even approach any-thing of the trip again so soon and besides, she rationalized, the grant has to get itself done first. First, the grant.

And what about her father? She was happy to know he was alive but didn't want to think about him at all, yet. As Erin had said, his silence spoke. Actual words might make the thing worse.

Easing on the brake for the stoplight just before the ABC store, she made a split second decision and swung to the left, onto A1A Beach Boulevard, which took her through a small patch of protected scrub, bird sanctuary and ocean-front, more or less devoid of human touch as part of Anastasia State Park. No one was behind her, so she slowed to a crawl to gaze at the Florida coast as it might have been if all the Floridians and their endless developments were suddenly sucked away, leaving the land to the birds and turtles, geckos and snakes.

"Just let me come back as a manatee," she murmured aloud as she swung the car around the curve onto Beach Boulevard proper, and left Old Florida behind to face, just beyond the St. John's County Fishing Pier, an inn on the beachside, a Key West style open bar restaurant on the other, and then another hotel, another bar, another and another, packed along the two-lane "Scenic and Historic Coastal Byway" all of them demanding the driver's attention: Best shrimp in town! Best view on the beachfront! Miniature golf! Children stay for free!

Slowing down, Claire pulled suddenly into a lot on Third Street, before a modest, almost shabby little building, painted a light mint green with cranberry trim, eyeing it warily, not sure, at first, if the tiny place could be anything other than abandoned, but it wasn't, of course, she'd heard people talk about the *Café Atlantico*. The owner and chef had transformed an old fifties filling station into a chic, Italian restaurant. In fact, she had probably driven past it literally thousands of times, but she'd never had the chance—or made the time—to try a meal there.

Nodding to herself now that she'd located the place, she backed out and continued on her way. When he had called again, just a day ago, to suggest they meet, perhaps have dinner, she had almost forgotten his first call, the one she'd called a prank, the one that had helped to darken her flight to San Francisco. But when he explained himself, it all became something quite other—

"Ms. Holt, please, you might remember my father—" he said just as she'd started to read him the riot act, how dare you, who are you—

"—Dennis Valery. I was named after my Uncle Jordan, Dad's youngest brother."

Claire found herself staring blindly out the window of her study, trying to see the older Valery, but she'd only met him, what, once? "Dennis Valery? His brother? The one whose car—" she started shakily.

"Yes, sadly. I was eight years old when it happened, but he was my favorite Uncle. Perhaps because I was named after him, I don't know, but I do remember him."

"Oh my God," said Claire. "Jordan Valery."

"Yes, ma'am."

He sounded so polite, so well-mannered and gentle, she agreed to meet him for dinner at the *Café Atlantico*—he happened to be vacationing in St. Augustine with his own wife and two kids, so he thought he'd try to meet the somewhat mythical—at least in his family—Professor Holt.

"I wonder if he looks anything like Jordan did back in the day," she said to herself as she pulled into the mall at the end of the Beach Byway and parked in front of the Publix grocery store. She yanked up the hand-brake and sat for a moment, distracted by the image of Jordan, her Jordan, his face so seriously focused on a pencil sketch he was doing in art class. It felt like eons ago, yet the image was as intense and precise as his sketches had been—*if he'd lived*, she thought, *I bet he would have been the artist he wanted to be.* Intense. It was something they shared. She shook herself, shut off the car, went and picked up a loaf of bread to go with the spaghetti and meatballs she'd planned for Ruth's supper and continued on her way back out onto the four lanes of A1A south, away from St. Augustine Beach, out toward Fort Matanzas.

At the 206 junction, A1A narrowed back down to two lanes, and the houses on the coastal side began to grow exponentially. One in particular loomed there, a cedar-shingle pseudo New England beach "cottage" which was nowhere near a cottage which belonged to some Hollywood actor, she could never remember which one. She drove over the Matanzas Bridge, where the usual complement of fishermen tried their hand and into Summer Haven, a tiny hamlet far less of a resort and more of a little town than many of those along the Palm Coast, although it had not escaped development.

Finally, she was out onto the road to the Whitney Lab, where development thinned the farther along she went, although just over the small causeway over the marsh there was this relatively new development, mammoth homes crowded cheek by jowl on tiny plots. Those houses still had the ability to make her sigh with regret remembering how it was when she'd first moved out there, only a few old pre-war and post-war homes, not these colossal pink, blue, powder-yellow South Florida transplants, many with a screened pool hardly ever used, or so it seem to Claire, who would've sworn she'd never seen a single person cavorting—or just swimming—in any one of them, ever.

The Whitney Laboratory sat upon the grounds of one of Florida's oldest tourist spots, Marineland. Built in 1938 as "the world's first Oceanarium" Marineland expressed the grandiose idea that America—no, the world—needed a museum of all the ocean's wonders. It didn't really work out and Marineland became a shabby quirk of the past until a massive re-building effort began to make the place viable again, as a marine life conservatory, dolphin sanctuary, research station and visiting center. Next to the ongoing construction, the Whitney looked, at least from the roadway, puny, unprepossessing, almost as abandoned as the *Café Atlantico* had looked, to Claire.

But of course about the Whitney she knew better: her lab was a hidden gem, or perhaps just a camouflaged pearl, made to seem drab and unexciting to the appetite of tourism. Inside lay a rich mélange of on-going investigations to whet the envy of any marine biologist worth the salt life.

Claire parked her aging Saab, gathered her things and went around back, to check up on the tanks, before heading to her office. Specimens collected locally and globally—most from the Caribbean—filled the dozen concrete tanks in an open-air lab space connected to the main building. The air inside was sea-pungent and today sped her back to the fish-shops her mother favored on the Jersey shore, where they'd go to pick out that rare summer treat, a live lobster. Setting her purse and papers on a stool, Claire walked briskly to a tank along the back wall where the horseshoe crabs were kept. She leaned over and caught a small male, turning him over. His spidery legs groped for a purchase, but all he caught was air. *Not your element*, she thought at the crab. *Sorry buddy.*

"Professor Holt?"

Claire nearly dropped the dripping horseshoe crab on her foot.

"Oh God, I didn't mean to startle you!" said a young man who looked a little familiar, but not very—he was on the short side, in blue-jeans, thin to emaciated, a freckled redhead with an uncombed mass of shoulder-length curls and dark, wide eyes. Gingerly she let the crab loose in the tank, shaking water from her hand. The young man went on hurriedly. "You see I'm one of the new graduate students this semester, and I haven't had the chance to meet you yet so when I saw you come in this way I just thought—"

"It's all right, you surprised me, that's all. I'm usually one of the few around the place on the weekend. What can I do for you?"

"I was hoping to talk—do you have a minute?"

Claire shrugged. "Sure. Come follow me back to my office, where we can sit."

"Thanks, really. I appreciate—"

"Not a problem—" she pushed open the door to the inside of the lab and headed up past the long prep tables, neat and empty for the weekend, with the graduate student at her heels. "And your name is?" she asked.

"Thomas. I mean, Logan Thomas."

"Hello, Logan Thomas. You can call me Dr. Holt. Or if you prefer, Claire."

"Thanks, Professor Holt."

One of the formal ones, she thought. "So, where are you from, Mr. Thomas?"

"California. I…um…can't get used to saying Doctor. At Cal, we said Professor or a last name. Porter. Thomas. Holt—like that—"

"How Navy. In the South, we say doctor. You went to Cal…?"

"Santa Barbara."

Claire whistled. "Expensive place—" by this time, they'd gone through the common lab, down the long, greenish hall and into her lab/office space, dark and crammed to the ceiling with things necessary, unnecessary and in some cases, forgotten, boxes, old lab reports, magazines, journals…she always meant to tidy up.

"Every fall," she said, "I promise to tidy the place and every fall the clutter just grows worse."

"Always looks the same to me," said Tessa, a research assistant, who was hunched over a microscope at the end of one of the two long lab tables. "Hi Dr. Holt!" she said brightly out of the gloom.

"Cramming, Miss T? Look who I found lurking about the salt water tanks."

"Yeah. Hi Logan," said Tessa. "I kinda told him you might drop in. He's been wanting to meet you."

"Have I been that hard to find?"

Tessa shrugged and went back to her slide.

Claire walked briskly to the back of the room, around a stack of folders, and boxes, and unlocked the door to her office. She beckoned Logan to have a seat in front of her desk, which sported piles upon piles of paper. Actually, the only thing not cluttered was the chair he took. She lifted some forms the department secretary had left for her to fill out and sat, put her purse under the desk, turned on the light, glanced at her phone—no messages—and then turned back to Logan.

"Have I really been that hard to find?"

He shrugged. "We seem to be on opposite schedules."

"Really—this place is so small, I would've thought…" she trailed off and folded her arms. "So. Just what can I do for you, Mr. Thomas?"

He cleared his throat, and glanced around the cramped office as if looking for an answer in all the academic debris, as he twirled the end of a red curl around his finger. "Ever since I started as an undergraduate, I've been following your research, Prof—Dr. Holt—and I came here, like, to work with you."

"Flattery so early in the game, Mr. Thomas?"

He blushed furiously, and let his long hair curtain his eyes. "No, excuse me, but no. I mean I understand it's not the best thing for a graduate student to do, go to a program just to work with a certain person—I was warned over and over that by the time I got here, you might have taken a job elsewhere. But you're here, and now I'm here and well—" he stopped, as if out of air.

Claire smiled. "You do flatter me, then."

His blush deepened, moving down to mottle his throat and he mumbled something she couldn't catch, took a deep breath and then said, "I'm sorry if I offended you. That was not my intention."

"And I didn't mean to embarrass you, Mr. Thomas. Really. I've never had a student seek me out by reputation alone. In fact I wasn't aware I even had a reputation, or something like one."

"Are you kidding?" He seemed genuinely astonished, and his blush blanched, as if he were a chameleon looking for cover in a snowstorm. He shook his curly hair back from his face. "I don't think anyone has done as interesting work as you have, not since Vickery's suppression PCR-enhanced subtractive hybridization helped his lab isolate that associated protease, you know, the one with a DNA sequence similar to plasmin?"

"Plasmin," Claire made a wry grimace. "If only we could get farther with that, eh? Compared to sea stars, humans have little power to regenerate tissue. We're pathetic! Can't replace lost limbs, heart muscle and nerve cells incapable of repairing damage."

"Which makes the work you've pursued all the more imperative." He blushed furiously again. "And mine. I mean, I don't want to brag or anything but I've been working with an asteroid we collected in the Gulf of the Farrallones—"

Claire sat up straight at the coincidence. "The Farrallons?"

"Yeah, last spring, I spent some time up there, kind of volunteering at the Sanctuary and had the good fortune to join a diving expedition—well, we were collecting, you know? A fishing expedition, and we found these unusual sea stars, very small, spiny, almost but not quite brittle, and of such a blue—lighter than *Linckia laevigata*, almost aquamarine, so they are nearly invisible, in the water and they're beautiful, Dr. Holt. We even got to name it!" His voice struck the ceiling. He lowered it. "It was an honor."

"Certainly. Go on."

"And this asteroid appears to share even more striking similarities in the very early stages of embryonic development to humans than other species, plus it has an immune response to injury that makes the common sea star seem, God, almost slow. And so I brought it—and me—to you."

"But I didn't see any new specimens in the salt tanks—"

He shook his head. "When I say small, I mean tiny. And fragile, extremely fragile—I didn't dare trust the communal tanks. They're too crude. I've got an aquarium in my cubicle. Actually it takes up most of the cubicle. And the great thing is that this building's on a generator."

"In Florida, we have to be. Hurricanes, you know."

He shrugged. "It's still great. Anyway I was thinking maybe that's part of the reason these stars have such a rapid and massive immune response, maybe for species survival. Even in a controlled environment, without predation, they don't reproduce larvae in quite the numbers other species do, but they can clone themselves, so a complete animal can be re-grown from one arm."

"The genus is *Linckia?*"

"Yep."

"I thought most if not all *Linckia* were tropical."

He scrunched himself up in the chair, crossed his ankles and frowned. "Usually."

"But you found this one in Northern California?"

His face became still. "You can guess what we all thought, can't you?"

She sighed. "Global warming."

He nodded. "The Gulf's tepid enough in certain places, now, to support them. That's the surmise."

"Great. We may benefit, or we may all drown, first."

"Yeah. And we'll be the first to go, here in Florida." He stood. "Would you like to see them?

"Of course, Mr. Thomas, please lead the way."

As they left her office, and threaded through the maze of her lab, down the green corridor and back to the graduate student's office cubicles, she found her heart beating another rumba, but this time it wasn't anxiety, or fear, but rather a pure adrenal rush, a surge, almost as if she'd taken hold of a downed, live power line—*now, could it be now and at last that the real work, will it finally begin—? How many times have I thought, this is it? But—*

"Mr. Thomas, besides my so-called reputation, what drew you here? I'm curious."

He said over his shoulder. "I meant what I said. You did."

"But really, I've been hammering away for twenty years, and haven't make a breakthrough, like Dr. Vickery's lab did with plasmin. You could have gone to the University of Alabama and studied with him."

Logan paused at the mouth of his cubicle, which had his last name provisionally tapped to the outer wall. He looked at her so hard she grew embarrassed and tried to gaze past him, or at least somewhere over his shoulder, as he said, "Tenacity. You are ferocious, Dr. Holt, can't you see that?"

"A ferocious failure," she said quietly. "Some would say foolish."

"No. You've worked in a vein that others abandoned and I just happen to think that you're right. I want to join that, be a part of it." He stepped back and swept his hand in front of him, like an old vaudevillian. "Madame, please to meet my little *Linckia.*"

She stepped past him with a giggle at his clownish bow. As he'd said, the shimmering tank nearly filled the cubicle. On the sand and rocky bottom lay bolt blue, infinitesimal stars, like a spray of tiny blue glass shards. One of these shards began to curl into more of a ball than a star. Claire crouched and nearly put her nose to the side of the aquarium.

"And just what, Mr. Thomas, did you name this beauty?"

"I—I didn't tell anyone else at the time, but we gave it my mother's name," he paused. "*Linckia claritas caerulus.*"

She looked an inquiry up at him. "Your mother's name is clear blue?"

He laughed and said, "No, oh no. My mother's name, like your's, was Claire."

When she cocked her head, he sighed and ran his hand through his hair, as his face contracted into the past. "I was sixteen when she was diagnosed. Pancreatic cancer. And, yes, she was also a ferociously determined woman. Even now, after all this time, I still can't believe she's gone."

Claire stood. "I know. Believe me—I do know. Only too well." She put her hand on his shoulder, mustering futurity and said, "Shall we get started?"

His face broke from the cloud of loss into a lissome grin.

In the evening light, *Café Atlantico* looked far more warm and alive than it had in the daytime, although still just one step beyond modest, its neon sign a single thread of pink and white light, the ramp leading up and around to the front door deliberately run-down, all done with an under-stated elegance. Any typical Florida beach tourist, seeking the best shrimp in town, best view, best BBQ would have driven right by, which was fine by Claire who admired how rust and peeling paint made for an artful distress; the exposed brick harkened back to the fifties; the metal front door looked like beaten copper left out in the sea air, and the restaurant's logo, a stylized, eight-legged octopus that also looked like a star had been etched into single frosted pane of glass. She pulled the door open; just inside was a miniscule teak and mirror wine bar to her left; on her right, a wall with a narrow table, on which lay sample menus and *Café Atlantico* business cards.

"May I help you?" The woman who spoke was a pretty, very spare blonde, with large, almond-shaped green eyes, whose hair was pulled back into a severe bun. Her dress was black, as were her mules, and her whole subdued demeanor and dress bespoke the same aesthetic as the restaurant, all of which Claire caught in the same split second in the thought, *she must be the chef's wife, lucky woman. She looks happy.*

"I'm supposed to meet—" she gazed quickly around the restaurant which was so small, it held only about ten or so two tops that she could see and by that time, Jordan Valery was already halfway across the one large room with his hand—his only hand, the other one was missing, except for part of a thumb and palm—held out.

"Professor Holt?"

"Yes—please, call me Claire."

The *maitre-de* and solitary waitress/chef's wife melted back behind the bar.

"Claire—" he shook her hand with warmth, as she looked him over, quick. He blushed slightly and said, "I take after my mother's side of the family, not my father's."

Claire laughed. "I'm sorry, an old woman's folly—"

"No, really, it's fine," he said, pulling out a wooden café chair for her. Sweeping her skirt carefully beneath her, she sat down. He took his own seat across from her, a broad-shouldered, heavy-set but not heavy African-American man, whose whole bearing bespoke military training or football, or both. "I think it's probably just natural curiosity. He was my Uncle, after all."

She nodded. "I'm afraid I don't recall your father. It all— that summer—it all seemed to happen so fast, and so slow. The longest summer in the history of the world, to me, I was so in love. And then it was over, Jordan Valery moved away, and by the time Inga was born, Jordan was gone."

His grave face became graver. "My grandparents moved the family to be closer to my father and mother. Jordan was their youngest child, an after-thought you might say, and they felt they couldn't handle him properly. They wanted my father you know, to sort of step in and give my Uncle a role model. Dad was career Army all the way, just out of Vietnam. Wasn't easy for him, but he did make it a career. And set an example." Pride put even more posture in his already impressive carriage. "When my best friend from high school and I went off together and joined up, he was beside himself with suppressed happiness." He said thoughtfully. "My mother's words, not mine. I can't ever remember seeing Dad crack a smile."

"Ah. I thought you might be in the military."

"You mean this," he gestured with what was left of his hand.

"Not exactly," she said, embarrassed. "You seem like an officer, to me."

"Why, thank you, ma'am. I try to be both an officer and a gentleman, for my own kids' sake. Two boys."

"And I have two girls—well, Inga is in her thirties, about to be a mother herself, and Ruth is just finishing high school.

And training for the Olympics—" she caught her breath. "I still can't believe it, every time I say it!"

"Your daughter has ambition—I know how that feels. I hope my boys have half as much as I did!" he said fervently. "They'll need it, in this world. I know I needed it."

Claire nodded and then took a moment to look around. The whole place was egg-shell white, except for the warm wood of the teak bar over which hung two paper-shaded pendants; the windows wore large canvas shades that had the feel of Asian sails, and echoed the white table cloths, and the neat, spare room was decorated with a few modern paintings under spots, one well-placed terra-cotta statue and one that looked like a porcelain Giacometti. Jordan, meanwhile, was scanning the slim wafer of a menu.

"How did you hear of this place?" she asked.

He looked up. "My wife's sister lives in St. Augustine— that's who we're staying with, in fact. She teaches at one of the high schools." He cleared his throat. "Actually, she was your daughter's English teacher last year, and a kind of unofficial guidance counselor of sorts—she gave your daughter some timely advice, or so she tells me."

"Ruth? What kind of timely advice?"

He shook his head. "My sister-in-law takes her confidences quite seriously. I don't know. But she heard quite a bit about Inga, too, and slowly the names rang a bell, she emailed me and, well, the minute I Googled you, I knew I had the right Claire Holt. But what I didn't know until then is just what sort of work you've been doing." His gaze became strangely intense. "After my fun with an IED—and I was the luckiest one in my platoon—I was given a pretty fair prosthetic hand, but it's really only for cosmetic purposes. I know it might sound strange, but if I'd lost more—well, you know there are some pretty fancy arms out there, and I hear there are even more advanced versions in the pipeline. It's okay, I mean I know I'm lucky, but to grow a new one—" he shrugged. "Five fingers, just like a starfish, so I just had to ask you, since we do have this family connection and all—do you think it is possible? In my lifetime, do you—"

She stopped him by gently laying her hand over his good one. "Jordan," she said and that old, beloved, bedeviling name did not come easy. She had to clear her throat. "Honestly? I don't know. I'll admit that I'm more optimistic tonight than I've been, well, in years—" she had to catch herself from offering false hope. The rush of her afternoon in the lab had acted on her like a strong upper. "But, I'm still going to say, I very much doubt it. I'm a scientist, and, well, it's difficult for me to deal with things that aren't facts. We're still a long way off."

He sighed, nodded and slipped his one hand out from under hers, to look at his menu again. "I had to ask."

"Of course you did." She lifted her menu too but closed her eyes, wishing with all her heart that she could've given him the gift he so wanted. *If only I'd been more successful,* she thought and the worry-stone weight in the pocket of her heart grew larger. *See what comes of failure, of not trying hard enough! So much for my reputation of tenacity, Mr. Thomas, but the blunt fact is, I've failed.*

With something like a profoundly keen insight that many waiters seem to have, their waiter appeared at that very moment to distract them both from the real and painful corner their conversation had painted them into.

"It's been raining for three solid days," Claire said to Max, long distance. "Darkness, rain, thunder. And it's freezing. I can't remember the last time December was this cold!"

"Oh really? It's ten below here," he said drily.

"All right, all right, you win! How's my sweetness doing?"

"Plump as a cherry," he said. "At the moment, fast asleep."

"Did my roses arrive?"

"One dozen hothouse long-stems, yes. Inga was delighted. I'd put her on the phone, but she's napping—"

"Oh, no, don't bother. Sleep is precious when you have a newborn."

"Newborn! She's already two months. I can't believe it—"

"Trust me, time keeps on getting speedier." She blew her nose. "Besides which, you two—no, you three—will be here for New Year's. I'm counting the days."

"How is that cold doing?"

She sighed, blew her nose again. "It's fading. I'm glad Ruth and I didn't try to travel, though. She had a worse version, although she threw it off faster than I seem to be able to do."

"Well, she is all of eighteen. Anyway, to be frank, Claire, I'm glad we split up the holidays this year, with the baby and all. My parents have missed you and Ruth, but this way, I think we will all enjoy things with far less stress. Travel has become such a nightmare."

"I know," she said, without muster, thinking as they said their good-byes *all things do come to an end. We will probably never get together again, not as we did last year.*

She sat at her desk in the studio staring at the phone, remembering that first holiday season after David's crash. Because he was Jewish, and she (well lapsed) Catholic, they'd celebrated both Hanukah and Christmas, modifying both a little from the rather lavish things their parents had done—Jane had been a true Christmas fanatic, and David's folks devout—so as not to be overwhelmed by the season. All her young life, Ruth had delighted in the mix, but without her father, as the holiday season approached, she grew mute, almost catatonic, and Claire, frantic, turned to Inga for help.

"Thank god for you, sweetheart," she murmured and picked up the framed picture of her daughter and grand-daughter at the birthing center that Max had sent to her, her tiny namesake looking appalled by the camera's intrusive flash.

That first awful holiday-season-that-wasn't-anything-without-David, Inga had insisted Claire and Ruth take a road trip up the coast, and the three of them would "do" New York City, like tourists from abroad. It had proved a tepid but adequate antidote to the tide of their loss, and while they could never quite dispel the vacuum David had left, eating a soft pretzel in the frigid winter air while watching the skaters on the ice in Rockefeller Center at least had not been home, full of memories, in the Florida sunshine.

Claire blew her nose again, stood up and went to the kitchen for some tea. The mail for the day had been delivered and was splattered all over the slate floor beside the front door. She bent to scoop it together, started sorting. The bills she put in a pile and left as she always did on the hall table, to be carried back into the study later. The rest she took with her into the kitchen, slipping most of it under one arm. First she opened a large manila folder with no return address.

"Dad?" she murmured, glancing at the signature on the short letter, which read:

Dear Claire:

I had hoped to hear from you before this; Debra said I should go ahead and write myself if I wanted, so here I am, writing. Not very good at this, though. Rusty. Inside the envelope you will find the first section of a diary my mother kept when she first married my father. My sister sent me two books out of five, when I said I would transcribe them for the family. Rather painful reading, but I thought you'd like to have it. Helga Green born Crane, my mother, had a grim time in her short life—but you will see. She's very honest with herself, and perhaps, in a way, it might help you understand what happened between your mother and me. I'll send more as I go.

Love, Dad.

Claire put the sheaf of papers down on the kitchen counter thinking, *I'll deal with that time-bomb later* and gratefully turned to opening the holiday card from Max and Inga.

"Oh my word," she breathed and started laughing. Inside the card was another photograph of baby Claire, dressed up as an elf or holiday sprite in spangled green tights, a tiny red jacket and a blue and white hat with a star of David instead of a pom-pom on the peak. But it was the expression on baby Claire's golden face that dwarfed the ridiculous nature of her costume by the utter serenity of her huge, dark moss green, almond-shaped eyes.

"You are a queen," Claire said to the picture, as she propped it up on the kitchen counter where she'd stood the other holiday greeting cards.

"I am?"

Claire turned around. "Ruth! But—I thought you'd be gone by now!" She glanced at the clock. "Shouldn't you be at practice?"

"Yeah, I guess—" but instead she sat the kitchen table with a bowl of half-eaten cereal. She tipped a little milk into her spoon and let it dribble out again. "Am I your queen?"

Claire smiled. "I was thinking of baby Claire, but you will always be my princess."

Ruth huffed. "Like, I'm not a baby anymore!"

Claire sat down at the table. "Honey, I know that. What's wrong?"

The teen-ager shrugged and dribbled another spoonful of milk.

"Well, when you do want to talk about it, let me know. Shall I drive you over to practice?" She glanced at her watch. "You'll only be a few minutes late."

Ruth dropped the spoon into the bowl. "I'm not going," she said and burst into tears, but pushed her mother away when she reached for her. Mastering her emotion, Ruth said, "It's just so unfair, like, and—" she set her mouth in an angry line "—and wrong. Plain wrong. But nothing I say stops it, nothing I do helps."

"What's happened?" asked Claire sharply.

Ruth shook her head. "It's not like that—like something happened, not exactly *happened*, you know. It's like—" she breathed out— "it's just there, all the time. Just there, and I can't stand it anymore. I can't, like, just ignore it and I can't, like, do anything."

Claire could feel the tension bending Ruth to incoherence, the atmosphere of the impossible robbing her of words. Carefully, Claire said, "You are doing something, though, Ruthie. By not going to practice, you are taking action—"

"Not what I really want to do! Like, I want to go. But I can't." Ruth wiped her face down with both hands, sprung up from the table and started kicking the window gently with the rubber toe of her black converse sneaker, her hands in the back pockets of her jeans, staring out at the pool, her face as tragic as if the pool itself mocked her.

Claire waited.

Ruth took a deep breath. "It's not blatant. You see? Not like the time you and your old boyfriend found that raccoon."

Claire's throat closed. She cleared it. "The one in the parking lot."

"Yeah. This whole thing just makes me cry!" And tears ran down her cheeks. She didn't bother to wipe them. "But the thing is, that raccoon, that was blatant. This isn't."

Now it was Claire's turn to take a deep breath and let it out, trying to lower the tension that fisted her hand. "Who isn't being blatant about hate?"

"My so-called teammates. Well, like, not all of them. Just three. But it's making me crazy, they act so sweet, but everything they say hits my ears one way and I can tell nobody else hears what I'm hearing."

"Because you're—"

"—Jewish, and darker than they are. I mean, I've had, like, problems with mean kids or cracker kids in school before, this is North Florida, we're in the South, not Miami. I'm not dumb, I know I don't have straight hair and a tiny button nose. But this…this is different—constant, secret, torture. I can't really tell Coach, he's their coach too, and besides he's—" she shrugged.

"What?" Claire paused and frowned. "He's white, is that it?"

"Maybe. I guess. Not really, though." Ruth shook her head. "It's more like he's just a *guy*, you know? I mean, he's great, a great Coach, that's not the problem. It's like—the air I breathe is heavier than the water I'm swimming in. The only relief is actually swimming when I can't hear nothing but pool."

"Shit."

"Mom!"

"Well? This is awful."

"Tell me about it."

Claire folded her hands in her lap to gain something like composure. "This shouldn't be happening."

Ruth rolled her eyes. "Duh."

"Why don't you let me come with you to practice today?"

"Oh yeah right, what good will that do?"

Claire shrugged. "Your Coach won't mind?"

"No, but, Mom what are you going to do?"

"Nothing."

"Then, like, I don't see the point!"

"Just go get your gear."

"Mom—"

"Trust me, Ruth. Besides, I've not seen you practice recently. It's about time."

In the car on the way to the pool, Ruth fidgeted, tapped her feet, put her iPod ear buds in, took them out. "Ma, what are you going to do? You've got that look on your face—Nana's look, you know, The Glare."

"Do I?" Claire glanced briefly into the rearview. "Well now I never noticed before. But you're right, I've got me a Mini-Glare."

"So? What are you going to do?"

Claire parked the car before she turned calmly to face her daughter. "Nothing. Ignorance can be a powerful force. I'll just let it work for me—us. When we get inside, as soon as you can, deliberately point out your three problems, I mean, make sure they see you point to them, then whisper in my ear. After that, just concentrate on diving."

"But—that is so high school," muttered Ruth.

"Of course it is." Claire laughed.

"You are like making me so nervous."

"Go on, Ruthie, just trust me."

"Whatever—" she opened the car door and almost shoved herself out; Claire followed her daughter to the Olympic-sized indoor high school pool. The close air was astringent with chlorine, and the sound of young voices bounced around, echoing loud. While Ruth went into the locker room to change, Claire exchanged pleasant greetings with the Coach and one other parent who'd come to sit on the sidelines until Ruth, suited up, returned; by that time, six girls and two boys were either in the pool, doing laps, or stretching. Ruth walked with obvious reluctance to her mother's side.

"All right, which ones—point, and point obviously. Be seen, but not by your Coach. I don't want out and out conflict."

"Please, Mom. It'll just get worse if you—"

"Which ones?"

Ruth nodded toward a clutch of three girls, one in the pool with her swim-cap on, the other two stretching, and chatting beside her. Since once they all put their swim caps on, it was almost impossible to tell one girl from another unless one was taller or shorter than another, Claire focused on a wiry girl with darkening blond hair and whispered to Ruth, pointing,

"That girl, what's her name?"

"Sheila Dyson."

Claire nodded slowly, and frowned. "Go practice, now. Just concentrate."

"But Ma—"

"Go on, sweetie. I'll stay right here." As if to prove it, she sat on the edge of a metal bleacher. "Try to have a good one."

Ruth shrugged angrily. "Like, whatever."

Claire nodded and turned her gaze back to the girl, Sheila, and left it there until the girl noticed—well, something. But Claire never let Sheila catch or return her gaze. This childish cat-and-mouse went on until the Coach called practice, and then Claire did not take her gaze off Sheila, nor did she care if her gaze was returned, or caught. After a few more minutes, Sheila started to frown; her diving form broke slightly, and suddenly her timing was off enough that the Coach shouted,

"Dyson! Where's your focus? Clean it up!"

Claire relaxed then, and shifted her attention to Ruth, whose third platform dive into the pool was a meticulous marvel, her honed young body a source of pride and *admit it, Claire, envy. You never, even at her age, looked so fine!*

Oh, yeah? You were pretty enough for Jordan though came unbidden out of the past, and it carried her back to that unusually frigid morning, early spring, so cold she'd dug out her mittens and matching crocheted hat, and found a sweater her mother had not yet sent off to the dry-cleaners in the back of her closet, so she could sneak out and meet up with Jordan, behind the high school in the teacher's parking lot. They'd been meeting there, regular, on Sunday afternoons, just to hang, and talk or pet and kiss, but she was nervous, this was all so new, and he'd been there before, with another girl, and she resented it and him for it *but he's so cute, just so cute,* she thought as she sprinted down the hillside behind the apartment complex, across railroad tracks, to the sidewalk up to the high school. She was late; he was already there when she came pounding around the corner.

"Jord, hey, I'm sorry—"

He had his back to her, and he was shaking a little, as if the cold had gotten to him so she came up behind him and put her arms around his waist, leaning her cheek against his plaid woolen jacket. After a moment, he pulled her gently around to his side and that's when she saw it, a raccoon, curled up at Jordan's feet, it's unruffled coat catching the afternoon light, it's bandit face closed in upon itself.

"Is it—?"

He nodded. "Some kind of poison. Look what they've done—" he pointed to a chalk circle drawn around the still animal, and the words *fucking coons fucking* scribbled inside.

"Oh my god—"

"Assholes. Douche-bags." He spat.

"But come on Jordan, who—"

His face grew stony. "You know who."

She shook her head. "I don't believe it. Tony wouldn't do something so dumb." She crouched down slowly, resisting her impulse to touch the creature, whose tiny, human hand-like paws had curled around each other, as if the animal were bowed over in gloved and sacred contemplation. "He's so… perfect," she whispered.

"Yeah, well, he should be fucking *alive*."

That memory snapped Claire back into to the present. A small tear formed in the corner of her eye. "So should you, Jordan. David—both of you. Alive." Angrily, she smudged away the desperately unwanted tear with her forefinger, and hugged her own elbows, as Ruth executed a nearly perfect pike.

Chapter Five

Love, Spring

Children's voices, some as high as abandoned shrieks, bounced around the room where the salt-water examining tanks made the air tangy as a fish-store after a fresh delivery. Kids clustered around two of those tanks, a rowdy, antsy group of second graders and a more glum cluster of teens, a few of whom affected, like, well, *to-oo-tally* bored boredom, as if they'd been doomed to a day in nerdville. Outside the large plate windows, a spring wind scudded fat, fleecy clouds across the marshland. Claire stood beside the windows, just inside the door of the examination room, and watched through the glass as a white crane unfolded; despite it's awkward size, the bird rose aloft with simple grace, angling in the wind. Claire felt her spirits rise a little on those ample wings, even if the loadstone in her heart kept her grounded.

With a half-smile, she turned around to the room and folded her arms, amused by the kids. Ever since she and two of her colleagues had started the K-12 outreach program at the Whitney, more and more of her afternoons had been spent welcoming the children and their teachers to the facility and then turning them over to Monica Greenway, the newly-hired director of the program, a former grad student who'd chucked the Ph.D. with relief. Not everyone was cut out to finish, and Monica had taken to her job with the kids as one who had, at last, found their calling.

"Here's our main hero of the day," she said to both groups, but her focus was upon the second graders, having left the teens in the capable hands of their own biology teacher, a middle-aged man with a shortish beard and longish hair, *a Mr. In-Between*, Claire thought—everything about him seemed utterly measured as he moved quiet among his charges; the teens of eternal boredom he ignored, for the most part, choosing instead to work intensely with the few whose attention was riveted by the sudden appearance of the main hero of the day—

"This is Houdini, one of our four resident octopuses," continued Monica, to the gasp of one child. In the tank, the ungainly yet dignified and unbelievably quick creature, let loose from a container Monica had transported him in, tentatively swept across the sand, like a woman in a flowing ball-gown, to vanish ripplingly inside a length of pipe. "We won't see too much of him but I'll put out some tasty bits to see if he'll show himself."

"Is he shy?" asked one child.

"Yes," said Monica. "Very shy. But also, well, very bold. We named him Houdini after he escaped from us for the third time. We have no idea how he got out of his home, but once we found him on the floor of the lab, once in the main hallway making for the door, and the last time we found him, he'd made it all the way to the road, heading with determination across the highway, to the open sea. We were afraid he'd get squished by a car, so we redesigned his tank—and so far, so good. But a Houdini can be very sly."

"What's ahoudini?" asked one of the smallest kids. "I don't get it."

As Monica began to explain the famous escape artist's exploits to a new generation, Claire found herself watching the biology teacher because he seemed familiar…and then had a instant of seeing herself, standing in the shower of her undergraduate-days apartment, memorizing declensions, etching into her reluctant head: *amo, amas amant*, as she brushed her teeth, teeth that were rattling with, well, lust for her T.A. He wasn't a particularly handsome man, her Latin T.A., but he had a quirky smile, large, mild and always sad brown eyes that many years later caught up with her in David's eyes, and a dry, wicked sense of humor, her favorite kind of humor, lashing, acidic, hysterically funny so long as you weren't the target of it. An Italian-American from Brooklyn by way of South Boston, Joseph—Joey—often tapped her shoulder after class, just to talk, or grab a cup of coffee or indulge in a wicked, useless shared passion for an ancient video game, *Asteroids*.

Claire shook her head. "What a waste of time," she muttered to herself, but she smiled, too, for the sheer remembered pleasure thinking quietly, *but love, in any form, is never a waste, is it?* Even as she panted for him, she'd also known that despite her all too visible desire, he'd keep their thing on the short side of paradise—young though he was, he was also a cautious and very married Catholic man. She unfolded her arms and sighed.

"That sounds like a sigh from the dinosaur days," said the high school teacher, whom she was startled to find standing quite close. He grinned through his short and she could now see, graying beard. "Surely you cannot be as jaded as my kids are?"

She laughed. "No, no, that would be impossible. I haven't as much hipness to uphold anymore—thank God. I watch my daughter try to keep up to the trend, what's the next sign of cool, and it's exhausting!"

He nodded. "One good thing about seeing the back of one's youth. Although as you can see, I spend a lot of time with the young."

"As do I," she said. "But I went for the college and post-college years. I didn't think I could handle the teens. Too much adrenaline plus hormones."

"You teach at the lab, isn't that so?"

"Yes," she said and put out her hand. "I'm Dr. Holt. Claire Holt."

"And I'm Dr. Starbuck. Dan Starbuck, and yes that's really my name, no relation to the coffee empire, no relation to the character in *Moby-Dick*."

"*Moby-Dick?*" She cocked her head. "Ooooooh-kay, whatever you say, Doctor."

He shrugged. "I did the Ph.D. but unlike you, couldn't hack the competition or the research. Just wasn't my bag. I started by teaching at a private school for boys but that sucked, and eventually wound up in high-school, mostly AP. I like the adrenaline and hormones, as you put it, so long as I can channel some of it—or rather, some of them. Excuse me, I see trouble—"

And he sauntered over to a little knot of his teens, who gradually unknotted, foiled by his genial presence. Whatever mischief the knot had tied itself to, unraveled as he approached.

Claire took that opportunity to leave the classroom and head back through the demonstration labs outside, across the exposed and wind-swept, sand and gravel parking lot to her own lab where Logan Thomas was preparing slides, his long red hair hiding his freckled cheek.

"You, sir, should take a break," she said. "Do you never sleep?"

He looked out from under his curls. "Not tired."

"Never?"

He laughed. "All right, always. Isn't that a given when you're doing a Ph.D?"

"As I recall from back in the day, yes." She mused for a moment, eyes closing. Back in the day, being a woman in the lab, too, had been grueling. *Had to prove yourself better than shit every single moment...*

"We're getting there, you know. I can feel it," he said.

She opened her eyes and smiled ironically. "Intuition?"

He leaned over the stool a little, and lacing his hands suddenly put them behind his head and shrugged. "Nah. Science." He grinned. "Okay, well, I'm going to knock off for the weekend soon."

"Do that," she said. "We've both been working too many hours."

He shrugged again, and although she meant what she'd said, she couldn't help but feel a little splurge of giddiness because as logical as she could be, she could feel it, too—they were somehow on the right track. Perhaps not in time to grow Jordan Valery a new hand, but maybe in time to help the children of his generation. She shook her head. *God forbid they will need it—maybe by 2025 there will be more more IED's?*

"Ha!" she muttered aloud. "Remember how you thought the end of Vietnam meant peace forever, you silly old thing?"

Unlocking her office door, she dropped her stuff on a chair, turned on the computer, checked her email, wrote a letter of recommendation, but as the afternoon passed, and the office darkened, she glanced up once to make sure she was alone, and then opened her bookmark to Petfinder.com. She hadn't gone to the site since she'd visited San Francisco, but for some reason, today, the thought of it had been jiggling in the back of her mind ever since she'd gotten out of bed. It was time.

On the search menu she chose dog, terrier, baby, small, male; the list that came back showed a number of mixed breeds, Jack Russells, Rats, and Pits, but on the third page she found a face that cried out to her "I'm your's, Claire! Please, please, come get me" a 4-month old male terrier mix, quite small, with prominent, even pop eyes, so big and brown (Pug?), mostly gray coat but a white beard (Schnauzer?) and a slight kink in the coat (Poodle? Schnoodle?) velvety-looking floppy ears (Yorkie?) and a pert snout (Shih Tzu?) with the overall effect of making Claire think "Toto!" (Cairn, like our clown, Rags?). His name was Cooper. He'd been rescued from an industrial garbage can near an I-95 off ramp in Fort Lauderdale. Perhaps it was his resemblance to Rags, or perhaps it was something about how assertive his nose seemed, or perhaps it was just love at first sight, but she emailed the shelter on the spot, filled out the online application and then couldn't wait, so phoned.

"What do you mean," she found herself shouting like a madwoman into the receiver, "you don't adopt out of state? I'm *not* out of state! I'm in St. Augustine—look, look, I don't care if you've had a thousand emails about Cooper! You can have the real me in the flesh. I'll drop everything and drive down there tomorrow, cash in hand, if I have to—"

Which is how she ended up the next morning long before dawn at the wheel of her battered old Saab, with a thermos of coffee, a hard-boiled egg sandwich, a new traveling crate, a new leather leash and collar. Backing out of her driveway in the dark, knowing Ruth was still sound asleep, Claire jogged the car over to I-95, destination Ft. Lauderdale, on what would soon become a hide and seek, cloudy to clear April morning. She drove with furious concentration, as fast as she dared which meant she kept the needle at around eighty and it was smooth, boring sailing past the Space Coast, to Ft. Pierce; there, she began to run into some traffic and too many thoughts—how she and David had found Buddy as a puppy, a full-bred Dalmatian, lost or left on her driveway; how no one had claimed him, as they held their breath, after dutifully putting an ad in the local newspaper, hoping no one would answer the ad—silence would be golden, in this case, said David—which made her think about Lulu and Erin, the tacit way in which none of the Three Musketeers had communicated after her trip: something had silenced them, and she was beginning to suspect it was time, the widening channel of time—*we've really been drifting apart for years*, she mused *but that last reunion snapped the connection.*

And then there was the still suspended business of her father. His silence, so long held, now had a small slit in it, since, for the past few months, he'd taken to calling her early Sundays, on her cell. She'd given him the landline's number, but he persisted in using the cell, as if the mobility and privacy of it consoled him. Or maybe he was just afraid to find himself talking to a granddaughter whose whole childhood he'd missed?

Their conversations were taut, awkward, gap-ridden affairs, having to do with daily things, like the insane price of gas, *but what did I expect? I just showed up on his doorstep, an unannounced ghost, just what did I expect?*

She shook her head, sighed and changed lanes as traffic began to crawl, yet still she managed to pull off I-95 by ten, to roll gratefully into a parking slot, right smack in front of Lauderdale Pet Rescue, a run-down facility crowded into a short strip of shops, tucked onto a sad outpost of a street sandwiched between the arch of the highway off-ramp, and square sets of dreary but brightly colored apartment buildings. She sighed, thinking *God, I hate South Florida* and pulled the hand brake. A little shaky, her shoulders stiff, she got out of her car just as a girl—or rather a young woman—opened the door of the shelter, with two small dogs together on one lead.

"I don't believe it—Cooper?" said Claire, incredulously, correctly—the smaller of the two dogs was the one she'd spotted on Petfinder. Responding to his name, the terrier sat back on his haunches, and lifted both front paws at her, as if in prayer.

"Goodness," said the dog walker, flustered. "Is he yours?

"Yes!"

"Really? Like, when did you lose him? I mean, we've only had him for like a week or so but he was in really bad shape when we found him, so we assumed he'd been abandoned, and for probably longer than a week—full of fleas, you know, skinny as skinny can be, his coat in mats, he was just covered with little nicks and scratches—"

Claire shook her head. "Who would do such a thing?"

The young woman, maybe twenty, gave Claire a suspicious frown. "I thought you just said he was your dog?"

"I'm sorry. I meant I do want him. I'm Claire Holt and I talked to—"

"You're the crazy lady from St. Augustine?"

Claire laughed. "I guess I do seem a little crazy."

"But like how did you get here so fast?"

"Determination and ignoring the speed limit. Can I pet him?"

"I guess…"

Claire crouched down and put her hand on the dog's flat gray forehead, a little taken aback by just how small he was—compared to Buddy, absolutely minute. Cooper responded by putting both delicate front paws on her shoulders and licking her face as methodically as if she needed a good and thorough wash. His whiskers tickled. Claire laughed, shook her head, rubbed her wet cheek on her sleeve and stood up, her every move followed by big brown pop eyes, soulful eyes, eyes that she would soon learn made people stop and say, "He's so cute! What kind of dog is that?" to which the answer was always: just a mutt, a rescue pup. If Cooper had a breed, it was unique unto himself, which is just another way of calling him—

"A terrier mutt," said the young woman. "We think mostly schnauzer. Well, if you do really want him, we'd better talk to Caroline, the director." She unlocked the door she'd just locked. "Hi. I'm Sherilyn."

By midday, after what Claire found an almost grueling round of questions, paperwork, once-overs, twice-overs, covert watching, phone calls, more questions and what not, *I'll give them a blood test if they want one* she thought at one point, as she sat in the shelter's little kitchenette, Cooper on her lap, waiting for some paperwork. *I'm not leaving without him* and then, finally Cooper was put into her arms for good, where he nestled with what seemed a knowing satisfaction as she whispered to his ear, "you got me, Coop, you got me now and forever, however long forever will be."

Several months after Cooper's adoption, Claire wondered how she'd ever lived without him. "Would you just look how the bees are flying about? I think they taste the spring in the air!" said Claire as she opened the French doors wide to the pool. "Maybe after the gym, I will just go and buy some gladiola bulbs for the garden—what do you think of that, Coop? Want to go to the garden shop with me? Huh? Huh?"

"Mom?" said Ruth as she wandered into the kitchen, the ends of her green cotton robe ties trailing on the floor. Cooper seized one end and tugged. Ruth tugged back. "Stop it, Rat-boy."

Claire turned around, put her hands on her hips. "Why do you call him that?"

Ruth tied her robe shut. "Terriers were bred as ratters, weren't they? And he'd sure kill a rat, like, if he could. He terrier-izes the squirrels."

Claire laughed. "So he does."

Ruth shook her head. "I'm going to have to tell Inga you've gone like totally batty. Loo-loo-loop-de-do, nattering on about nothing to a dog."

"Oh come on, now, Ruth, I used to talk to Buddy."

"Not the way you talk to Rat-boy."

"Meaning?"

"You *spoke* to Buddy. You *baby* Rat-boy. Since when did you become mommy to a dog? You were never Bud's mommy."

"Gracious, don't tell me that at your advanced age you're jealous of a puppy?"

Ruth shrugged. "I'm just saying."

Claire eyed Cooper, who eyed her back with what she swore was true sagacity. "I can't help it. He's so…himself. Come here, you little scamp!" Cooper dutifully trotted over in his own bouncy way and sat at Claire's feet. "Are you smiling at me?" she asked the dog, and then picked him up, only to get her nose fully licked inside and out.

"No French kissing please," she admonished, wrinkling her dampened nose.

"Ew," said Ruth. "Gross."

Claire glanced over at her daughter. "You know he aims for the mouth."

"I know, and it's like totally gross. And he may be sweet but he's also pugnacious," said Ruth. "And utterly bonded to you, like with super-glue. He's like so clearly the alpha dog around this house. You spoil him beyond spoiling."

"And I didn't spoil Bud?"

Ruth shrugged. "Whatever. Buddy ruled. Rat-boy has conquered. Are we going to see Nana this afternoon?"

"It's Sunday. Of course."

"Can I invite Harris?"

Claire put the dog down slowly, thinking fast. When she gazed back up at Ruth, she said calmly, "Do you really think that's wise, Ruth? You know I, myself, have no objections. You and Harris seem to get on well together, and of course I'm all for both of you, but you know I can't vouch for Nana, or change her mind. The last experiment—well. Are you sure you want to put poor Harris through another wringer?"

Ruth cringed. "No. But I do want him to understand me. I don't think anyone can understand me, you know, like really, without, like, seeing Nana. Seeing who she is. Or was."

"Was," said Claire softly. "You knew her as she was, and when she was still herself, sweetheart. Now, there's only a smidge of my Mother left to us both. And a lot of that bit of her is pure anger. You can see she's gotten much worse in the last month or so, can't you?"

"Don't say that."

"I'm sorry. It's the truth."

Ruth began to cry. "No." She turned her head, sheltering herself from her mother and ran out of the kitchen. Cooper sat down, watching the young human with mild surprise, as if to say, "Well now, what's this all about?"

"Time," said Claire. "A concept you, my Cooper, are mercifully without—memory, but no memories. Lucky you."

She put one hand on a hip. "Ruthie's right. I've gone around the bend. I'm talking to a dog." She bent down and picked Cooper up, touched her nose to his. "Do you think I've lost it, Rat-boy?" Cooper licked her nose again. She put his four paws back on the kitchen floor and he trotted away, in search of hidden treat or toy, just as she heard the muffled ringtone of her cell go off. She unzipped the outside pocket of her gym bag.

"Dad."

"Hi, Claire."

"Hello. Just thought I'd call."

"Uh-huh. And how has the week been treating you?"

"Fine. Retirement bores me a bit."

"Yes, I know, so you've said." *About six thousand times*, she thought. "And what do you feel now about my suggestion?"

"I don't think I can do it, Claire, I mean I can barely believe you have children, never mind grown children. To me, you'll always be my little girl. Did the photograph I framed for you arrive safely?"

"Yes, in fact it's sitting right here on the counter. It came in yesterday's mail." She wedged the phone between her shoulder and ear, and lifted the picture out of a torn box, a large color photo of herself, sitting on a swing, her head bent to one side, her gaze turned inward, a girl, around eight, make-believing to herself.

"It's my favorite picture of you."

"I see," she said, thinking, *what on earth am I going to do with a picture of myself as a child?* "Was it taken in the back yard?"

"You remember!"

"No, not really."

"Oh. Well. Did you open the other envelope yet?"

"What enve—oh. I see it." She fished a manila envelope out from behind wads of newspaper. "More diary?"

"Yes," he said, his voice going a little rough. He cleared his throat. "When I offered to transcribe it, I had no idea exactly how awful my mother had felt, to be so caught between the races in a no man's land…I mean, I can see why none of the family has wanted to travel back there, my poor mother suffered so much, was so angry and yet defeated, too—"

Claire felt herself freezing up again, as she did, now, whenever he seemed to want her sympathy—which had been a lot of late. *He doesn't deserve it*, she thought which came out as, "I know, Dad. Listen, I'm sorry but I was on my way out—"

"Oh, don't let me keep you."

"I'm sorry. I'll call you soon. Maybe you'll change your mind about a visit?"

"Okay, Claire. Talk to you soon." He hesitated. "Love you."

"Bye Dad," she said shortly, thinking '*I love you Dad*' *will not pass these lips ever again*. She snapped the phone shut a little too hard, stuffed it in her pocket and lifted the gym bag to her shoulder, thinking *coward. How sad, your own father nothing more than a self-centered coward*. She shook her head and opened the fridge for a bottle of water. *Don't be so hard on him, Claire. Some people would say your mother had been the coward, turning her back on her people as she did, passing for someone she wasn't.*

"You are both to blame," she said aloud, which startled Cooper into an inquisitive bark. She turned. "It's all right, my little man. Mommy has to go out for a bit. You be good, take care of the homestead. Ruth? Ruthie?"

A muffled "what?" came from her bedroom down the hall.

"I'm going to the gym. Be back in an hour or so."

"Okay."

"You okay?"

"Yeah, yeah. I'm busy. Texting Harris, Mom."

"All right. See you soon."

And she headed for the garage. About a week after adding Cooper to her life, she'd joined the Anastasia Athletic Club as another way of getting out of the house, of being, as Inga has put it, less of a lab-hermit. Walking the dog was one way; going to the Club another. Sure, she could always lift hand-weights and swim at home, but the Club gave her other options—spinning, pilates, tango lessons and people. Admittedly, many of the members were closer to seventy than fifty, but still she had managed to meet two new women friends: Nell, a widow, who had a son living far away in Ontario; and Kerry, a fierce lesbian—it was always the first thing she told you, "I'm a Lesbian, get used to it"—who taught film at the University of Florida and commuted because she couldn't stand the insularity of a college football town and, as she put it, needed the beach like a sea-turtle did. Claire smiled to herself because she thought Kerry looked, in fact, a little bit like a sea-turtle, being mostly round, despite vigorous work-outs.

As she pushed open the Club's doors, she scanned the lobby for either of her new friends, but was disappointed, so headed round a corner to the women's locker room and nearly collided with someone—a man—in swimming trunks, with a towel around his neck. "Excuse me!" she murmured, intent upon her workout.

The man touched her shoulder briefly. "Claire? Or should I say, Dr. Holt?"

She looked at him, puzzled. "I'm sorry—"

He looked a bit hurt. "Dan. Dan Starbuck. We met at the Whitney? My kids were on a field trip—"

"Oh, yes! Sorry! Out of context. I mean, you are." She blushed, feeling foolish. "Or I am." She put out her hand. "Nice to meet you again."

His handshake was brief and firm and she couldn't help but notice his wide, bare chest, toned—*he must lift*—under a heavy thatch of graying hair, a man of compact well-preserved strength, who knew what he had and how to make the most of it.

"Likewise," he said. "I didn't know you were a member?"

"I've only been one a short while."

"Ah, of course. Otherwise, we surely should have run into one another—small townism, and all, here in St. Aug. How are things at the lab?"

"Fine," she said, made vaguely ill at ease by his sheer, half-naked physicality. "Did your kids enjoy their outing?"

He laughed. "The ones who care about school did. The Whitney outreach program, though, has become a great asset to all of us teachers around here, as I'm sure you are well aware."

"I know, but it's always nice to hear it. On your way to the pool, I see."

"Twenty laps a day." He leaned up against the wall and folded his arms. "Much of a swimmer yourself?"

"No, even if water is my element."

His thick eyebrows shot up. "Your element?"

She smiled. "A manner of speaking. I love the water, but I can't swim. I dog paddle. It gets me from one end of the pool to the other."

"Can't swim? Oh, please. It's easy. I could teach you in a heartbeat."

He's flirting, she thought. *Is he? Oh dear*. Her gaze darted around. *Where's Kerry the sea turtle when I need her?* Smiling politely she said, "No thanks. To be honest, I've a pool at home, so I can swim to my heart's delight. I'm really here for spinning class." She looked at her watch. "Which has already begun. If you'll excuse me?"

He made a self-mocking half-bow and stepped to one side. Sheepishly, feeling as if she'd been churlish, Claire hurried into the locker-room, changed and scurried off to the spinning class. But she couldn't concentrate. And the teacher's choice of music—not a song she recognized in the bunch. It put her off. She quit the class early, showered and left for the lab. In her office, an email caught her off-guard and riveted her with tension before her computer, reading fast through a post from Erin titled: **The Noreen Report.**

Dear Claire:

You've been in my thoughts, and I've been meaning to reconnect but afraid, after all this time, to try. Yesterday, though, I got a call from Norrie's sister that she was taken by ambulance to a hospital. Rose got a worried call from the boys, who had found their Mom in her bed, gray-faced and panting. Where was Jim? Too drunk to notice. Anyway, it seems Nor had been battling a head cold which had morphed rapidly into pneumonia. She's in the ICU, recovering. I thought you would want to know. That nudged me to finally write this e-mail. I'm not even sure I have current contact info for you, or that you'd be interested in meeting up again. I know I can be difficult, sometimes. I natter on, for one (though Nor can give me a run for my runaway mouth.) But anyway if you would like to get in touch again, please let me know.

Erin

With an intensity that made her fingers dance on the keyboard, she emailed right back, asking for more information, if and where she should send a note or flowers and for a few moments, they e-chatted in real time; she was relieved to find out that Joshua had decided not, after all, to join the Marines; that Erin was indeed engaged to be married to my Mr. Free-Lance Catholic Boy, as she called him, and Lulu was fine and that despite the gulf of time, affection held. She sent off a picture of Cooper, ordered flowers on FTD for Noreen and then hand wrote a note to go with, adding at the end, *you might want to save this letter, as a relic of the past. I don't think anyone writes by hand anything anymore. Just call me old-fashioned. Love you & pray to see you soon, get well now, Claire.*

"Dr. Holt?"

She looked up. Tess peered around the doorframe.

"What's wrong?"

"It's Logan—I think he's sick."

"What?" Claire pushed away from her desk. "Where is he?"

"In the lounge."

Without more words, the two women hurried out of the darkened lab, down the hall and into the student lounge. Logan lay with his back to the door on an old grayish-yellow vinyl couch, torn and split, that had been in the lounge since forever; Claire touched his shoulder and looked into his face. He was asleep or more than asleep; she felt his forehead and found him cool.

"Get me some water, would you, Tess?"

"Is he all right? I couldn't wake him."

"No, but I think he's all right. Water?"

"Sure."

A moment later his eyes popped open and he pushed himself up. "Dr. Holt?" he murmured, his voice thick with sleep. "What are you doing here in the middle of the night?" He swung around to a sitting position and rubbed his face with both hands, one cheek creased with red lines from an old pillow, his shirt rucked and rumpled.

"It's hardly the middle of the night," said Claire. "In fact, it's just gone five in the afternoon."

He raised his head, his eyes penny round. "It can't be—"

"Logan!" cried Tess as she came back in with a bottle of water. She sat down on the couch next to him. "Are you okay?"

"Sure—" he yawned and stretched cattishly. "God, I must have slept all day."

Claire smiled. "Then you must have needed it."

Like a little boy, he rubbed his eyes and pushed the hair back from his face, which showed he'd not shaved in recent memory. "Ya," he said, swallowing another full body yawn. He gazed up at her, wonder blooming in his eyes, transforming a sleep-drugged face into a sharply focused and ecstatic one, as he said, "Come see what's happened. I mean we know how a post-traumatic-stressed asteroid shows a time-dependent increase in Hsp70 levels within 24 hours of amputation, but..." He bounced to his feet as if a human pogo stick and grabbed her by the shoulders. "I couldn't have slept like that until — come, come see—" and he took her hand, dragging her off like a brother would his little sister to some particularly intense form of play, with Tess trailing behind, back to the lab where the blue *asteroidea,* in various stages of amputation and re-growth, now glowed in small, separate tanks. He peered into one of the tanks. "These six. These are the six that grew into fully formed adults, from just the tip of one arm of the same star with a specific blend of chemical prompt and stem-cell enhancement—I mean I tried other combinations with no success." He looked over his notes, nodding, as Claire sat down in his cramped space and began, methodically, intensely, to go over his findings.

After about an hour, she turned to his anxious waiting face and said, calmly, "I'm going to need more time with this."

"Meaning?"

She shook her head. "I don't know—it looks…so prom-ising…and let me just say *we* didn't do this, Logan, you did it—I—" she leaned back, her voice crackling as she said, "If, after all these years—you've made—" Theatrically, she threw out her hand as a salute and said giddily, "—my Galileo, my Newton, hell, my Watson and Crick—"

He took her hand in both of his. "We did this, Dr. Holt. Do you hear me? Us. We did this together, working together." He glanced down at the little stars, glowing with their promise. "If we did anything at all."

One hot and darkening late August afternoon, Inga, nursing, carried baby Claire over to the couch in the living room. Gramma Claire, with Cooper curled in her lap, and Daddy Max, working at a bowl of popcorn, were sitting in front of a new flat-screen TV. The baby gurgled, sucking hard.

"Have you spotted her yet?" asked Inga.

Max shook his head and scooted over so his wife could sit down.

"The 10m women's preliminary platform is just starting."

"I still can't get over how sculpted she's become," said Claire. "All of them, just look at them, such carved bodies! I mean, she's always been thin, but now? Makes me feel like a doughnut."

"Mmm," said Max. "A doughnut sounds good."

"You don't need one," said Inga, digging an elbow into his side.

"Ouch."

"My god there she is, big as life!" cried Claire, who found the new high-def flat-screen picture Max had helped her mount on the wall unnerving, it was so sharply immediate. "How can she look so calm? Oh, my—this is awful. China. So far away! I should've gone with her. I should be there."

"Ruth is not calm," said Inga. "Trust me. And she wanted to go it alone, Mom. She's a big girl now, a woman, really. You need to let go."

"Yes, yes, of course," murmured Claire nodding, her eyes on Ruth as she appeared and vanished, depending on the camera and the angle. Wearing one of the new, astonishing aerodynamic swimsuits with which the U.S. team had been equipped, her clipped curly hair hidden under the sleek bathing cap, she looked more like an alien or maybe an otter—*that suit certainly leaves nothing to the imagination* Claire thought, *another Nana Jane saying, from the past, and yet what could one imagine?* Ruth had honed herself to such a diving blade so not to carry an ounce of extra flesh and when she cut the water after her backward 3.5 somersault pike, not a bubble rose.

"Oh, man, that was good," breathed Inga.

But the judges didn't think so. "Eight, Nine, Nine…"

Commentary buzzed in disappointment as the score went on.

"Eights and nines? That's all?" shouted Max, in outrage. "Give me a break, that was more than clean. Where are the 10s?"

Claire leaned back on the couch, every molecule of her body singing, *no!* her hand, once flat on Cooper's back, now clenching as she watched her daughter's televised face contract, then smooth out, in a new stoicism more akin to her sister's than to her usual waterfall of a wailing self. The dog sighed, stood, stretched, shook himself indignantly at being so ill-treated, and resettled.

For a few moments no one spoke, as the preliminaries continued.

Finally, Claire made herself say, "She can't medal, can she? I mean, that's the end, right there, that score, isn't it?"

Max shook his head, stood and nearly threw the remote at the television as he turned it off. "All that time, all those hours, all that work—and it's gone, all in a moment of failed judgment. My God. Heartbreaking." He sat back down. "Poor Ruth."

"Don't," said Inga, wiping the baby's mouth. The little one smacked her lips, beginning to fall asleep. "Look, she made it to the team. She made it over there. That's all that counts." But Claire could hear tears in her elder daughter's voice.

"I should have been with her," she said again. "For comfort."

Inga sighed. "Ma, how many times do I have to tell you she didn't *want* you there? Besides what would Cooper do, without his Mom? You know he sulks when you got to the bathroom, for God's sake."

Claire sighed and began to gently stroke Cooper's back again, which made him let out a big sigh himself, and a little moan.

"You see what I'm saying? He's got you wrapped around his little paw-paw."

"I know."

"My God," said Max again, shaking his head.

"She'll be all right," said Inga, trying to pull herself together. "So, Ma," she said, clearing her throat. "I've been meaning to ask what do you think of Barack Obama, now that he's taken the nomination?"

Claire roused herself. "Maybe we should call Ruth?"

Inga shook her head. "Let her call us. When she's ready."

"Oh. Well. Then. What did you just ask me?

"Obama. What do you think of him?"

"*Obama*? Well, I don't know yet. I like his wife. But I still think Hilary a better choice for the party—"

"Oh, Mom, you don't!" Inga shook her head. "I thought you'd be excited, a black man of your generation. You could've gone to high school with him. Or college."

"True," said Claire, reaching over for a handful of popcorn and munching it slowly, hoping it would help calm her, help her resist dialing Ruth's cell. "Still, I've also hoped for years to see a woman take that office. Anyhow, I'll make up my mind when Mr. Obama chooses a running mate. I want to see what kind of a decision he makes. That'll tell me more." She brushed her hands together, and lifted her arms. "Let me hold my namesake, please."

Inga looked down at the child, fast asleep. With care to jostle as little as possible, she handed the baby over. "She's a sound sleeper for which I am terribly grateful."

"Takes after me, when I was younger," said Claire, cradling little Claire. Cooper raised his head and stared at his human, with a look of righteous indignation. "Sorry, Coop. You have to share." The dog let out a snort. Claire laughed, quietly. "You know who has really inspired me of late, Max? Not Obama, although God knows it's about time someone other than a white man ran the country."

"What, you didn't think Bill was the first black President?" Max teased.

Claire gave him her best mini-Nana-glare. "You know what I think of that man."

"So whose inspired you, Ma?" asked Inga. "Your grad student?"

Claire's expression became solemnly bright. "Logan will take a Nobel someday. Mark my word, he's so gifted—" She smiled at her daughter. "Maybe we will make childbirth obsolete after all!"

"You're joking, I hope."

"Of course I'm joking. And yes I'm proud of him and happy to be working alongside someone who, yes, does inspire me in a way I've missed. It's almost like being in graduate school again myself—without the drama and the drain of it."

She shook her head. "He's given me back a certain kind of deep-seated joy I've been missing for quite awhile."

And yet, she thought, *that worry stone is still filling up the pocket of my heart, a hot little electric stone of—what? I wish I knew.*

"Careful," said Max. "You don't want to be caught robbing the cradle as my Chair always says."

"Oh, please," said Claire, dismissively. "I'm not in love with the boy. But you must know how it is, Max, when the delight of your field, your life's work, suddenly re-animates, suddenly lunges at you when you thought it had flat-lined?"

"Oh, yes," he said. "I know."

"But it's not Logan I'm talking about. The person I'm talking about is the Olympic swimmer, Dara Torres. Imagine steeling yourself to such discipline, to come back like she has, and go to the Olympics, at forty! Watching her, I was so inspired I started weight-lifting again."

"Really?" said Inga, cocking her head in exaggerated disbelief. "Are you sure that didn't have more to do with a man named Daniel Starbuck?"

Claire blushed, and turned her face toward the sweet and sour scent of baby to hide her embarrassment. "He's persistent," she murmured, so low she knew only the baby could hear, if she were listening. "I'll give him that much."

"What was that?" asked Inga.

Claire looked up. "I said that Daniel Starbuck is a stubborn man."

Max laughed and stood. "Come on, Cooper, we boys need to stretch our legs."

The dog's head bobbed up at the sound of his name.

"He looks just like a startled turkey, with his beard all mashed flat like that," said Inga. She stood too, and gently relieved her mother of the baby. "She's so out, I think I'll just put her down until she wakes on her own." She gazed into Claire's eyes and said, "I think you do like this man, though, Ma, don't you?"

Claire smiled. "Yes, I do. I like him. I hope you will, too."

Inga smiled, rocking the baby and winked. "We shall see. In the meantime, don't worry," she said. "Your secret is safe with little Claire."

Left quite alone in the living room, big Claire frowned to herself. Daniel Starbuck had been more than stubborn. He simply refused to either notice her chilliness, or to be bothered or flustered by her, no matter how often she'd refused his advances. Lately, he'd taken to bumping into her on the stretch of beach across the street from her house, since they didn't, it turned out, live that far apart, so she'd finally given in, gone on a couple of nice dinner dates. That night, he was supposed to come dine with them, and meet the visiting Northern half of the family.

She sat and toggled on the TV again, punching in the number for the Weather Channel. Tropical Storm Fay hung out in the Atlantic, threatening to reach hurricane force, and she waited to see the projected path, which, when it did come up on the screen, made her sit, then stand up. Fay would make landfall near Marineland. She went swiftly from the living-room, through the kitchen and out to the pool, to scan the sky, which was a dull to grayish white, flat, unyielding to sure interpretation. The breeze was stiff, but not yet a wind. Going back inside, she picked her cell up off the kitchen counter and called the lab.

"Hi, Dr. Holt. What up?"

"Hi, Logan. Honestly, will you never call me just Claire?"

He chuckled. "Nope. Just can't."

"Well. Have you been watching the weather?"

"Yeah, I don't think it'll be a problem."

"It might be, if it makes landfall near the lab."

"I thought this thing wasn't a hurricane."

"It isn't. Yet." She pursed her lips. "But it already has a name. That means it's near hurricane strength. You've never been through a really bad one, have you?"

"Nope."

"Mmm. Tell you what—I'll come down and bring a few *Linckia* home, just to be on the safe side."

"But we're on a generator—"

"Sure, I know. So is my house. Better safe than sorry," she said. "See you in a bit." She hung up and dialed her mother; as the phone rang, Max came in with a soaked dog at his heels. He took a kitchen towel out of a drawer and began drying Cooper's paws.

"Looks like rough weather ahead," he said.

She put a forefinger to her lips and nodded. "Ma? Hi."

"Claire, how nice. Are you coming to visit today?"

"No today. There's a tropical storm watch—have you seen the weather channel?"

"Oh, dear me, no, of course I was watching Ruthie, weren't you? My poor Dolly Dimples—and those foolish judges! It's so unfair! She was magnificent, beautiful. So strong." Jane's voice cracked.

"I know," Claire murmured.

"Have you heard from her yet?"

"No. Inga says when she's ready to talk about it, she'll phone. In the meantime, I think we should keep an eye on the weather."

"Do you think it will be that bad?" Jane raised her voice. "Vicki? Turn the television back on, please, dear?"

"Who is Vicki?"

"New night nurse." Jane lowered her voice to a whisper. "I like this one, she's got some spunk to her. Not like that other one, the thief who took my sweater. My *yellow* sweater."

Claire sighed. "I'm glad you like Vicki. I'll call later."

"All right. Love you."

"Love you, too, Ma."

"And how is Nana today?" Max asked.

"She sounded pretty good—well, except for Ruth."

"Ga!" he said, disgusted. "I'd like to give those judges a piece of my—"

"Listen, Max, I'm going to run over to the lab for a few things. I don't like the look of the weather at all, and I want to make sure everything's as safe as it can be."

"No problem. Need help?"

"No—well, if you'll amuse Cooper, or at least keep him company while he sulks? Inga's right, you know. He pouts if I close the bathroom door. To tell you the truth, when I'm alone in the house, I just don't close the door."

"TMI," he said.

"What?"

"To much information."

She laughed. "I see. Sorry. And if Ruth should call—"

"I don't think she will," said Max, frowning. "Not tonight."

Surprised, Claire said, "Why?"

He shrugged. "Absorbing what happened? She's not a talker."

Claire stared at him, as if he'd spoken a revelation. "That's so true."

"Hadn't you noticed?"

"Oh, yes but now that you say it aloud….and you know, Max, in all this time she's never really talked to me about David. Never. If I even get near to him in conversation, she grabs the steering wheel and veers us off." Her throat tightened, and for a split second a swell of conflicted, unusually powerful emotion broke over her.

"Claire?"

"Sorry." She caught her breath, trying to re-orient. "I didn't know until just now that Ruth's express silence on that particular matter had been gnawing at me."

"Maybe you should sit down? You look, I don't know, wobbly."

She shook her head. "No, I need to get to the lab before Fay gets any worse."

"Isn't it still a tropical storm?"

"For now." She smiled but it felt more like a grimace. "I won't be long."

By the time she reached the Whitney, though, the flat white sky had begun to bruise in the distance, a sickly yellow cast over a purple indigo, spreading. The breeze had become wind. Reaching her office, she booted the computer up and checked weather.com. Fay's projected course took her right over Marineland.

"Good God," she breathed, staring at the storm tracker. "She's got a bead on us."

Logan appeared in her doorway. "She does?'

"Looks like it."

"Well, here," he held out a specimen jar with a dozen or more live sea stars burning blue. "After you phoned, I collected them. Save some time."

She nodded. "Right," as he put the jars carefully on her cluttered desk. She roamed around the office until she came up with a box, put one jar in it, a piece of cardboard and the other jar, so they wouldn't clash and perhaps break. "Logan?"

He scratched his head. "Yeah?"

"Go home. The lab isn't hurricane proof."

He chuckled. "Is anything, really? Not my condo, for sure. Hell, lab's probably safer than the condo."

She stared at him for a moment then made a quick decision. "If that's the case, you're coming home with me," she said.

"Oh, no, Dr. Holt, I couldn't possibly—"

"Claire," she said, cutting him off. "We'll stop at your place for whatever you want. If Fay becomes a hurricane, I want to *know* you're safe. Best way is for me to keep my eye on you."

He hung his head. "Come on, it isn't going to be—"

"One night at my place won't kill you, will it? No. But a real hurricane could."

He laughed half-heartedly. "I'd be imposing."

"Hardly."

"You've family visiting."

"It's a big house. You can have the study all to yourself."

He shook his head. "I couldn't. Really."

"Wait a minute—don't tell me you can't stand dogs?"

He made a face. "No, I like dogs."

"Well, then, you haven't met Sir Gary Cooper. He's grey and white and love all over. Hurry up and say yes, Logan. *Linckia* needs its tank."

Whenever the doorbell would ring, Sir Gary Cooper always became completely hysterical, on full terrier "code red" no matter who stood on the threshold.

"Would you hush yourself?" said Claire, nudging the dog aside with an ankle and opening the front door for Daniel Starbuck, waiting, with his hands in his pockets, looking bashful through his beard.

"Um, hi," he said. "Hi, there Coop. You know me, don't you, your boy from the beach? Sure you do I've been here before. Come and have a sniff of your boy," but the terrier was already busy nosing his sneakers, checking out his ankles.

"How was the drive over?" asked Claire.

"Okay. Wind's intense, but no rain yet. What's the latest forecast?"

"We're still a bull's eye for this thing. Or rather Marineland is. Come in, before it does start to pour."

He shuffled over the threshold, trying not to step on the dog.

"Cooper," she said. "Give your boy some room."

But Cooper stood stiff-legged, hackles up, letting out a bark then a bay as if defending the castle from a full-scale invasion.

"Cooper!" scolded Claire, scooping him up off the floor, where the bark-bay huffed down to a deep-throated and suspicious, woof. "Sorry," she said to her guest. "You know how he's overly protective."

"More like jealous, I'd say."

"That, too."

"What's all the ruckus out here?" said Max. "Oh, hello!" He put out his hand. "Daniel, is that right?"

"Dan, please," he said, shaking hands. "You must be Max."

"Come in, come in—don't let our resident attack dog bother you."

Claire put Cooper back down on all fours and he followed the humans from the hall into the living-room, and then to the kitchen. Baby Claire lay in her stroller, kicking up at some bright rings and toys suspended there for her pleasure while Inga peered into a bamboo steamer atop a wok on the stove.

"Smells divine," said David after being introduced to Inga and the baby.

"Don't credit me for the divinity," said Inga, shrugging. "I'm just the *sous-chef* and scullery maid. Mom's the cook. I hope you like Chinese—"

"You mean Pan-Asian," interrupted Max. "Some of these spices seem suspiciously Thai. Like that fresh basil I found hanging out in the fridge."

"Isn't basil Italian?" said Dan.

"Pan-Asian, Asian-fusion," fussed Claire, pushing Inga aside playfully. "I follow my favorite chef's advice—mix it up. A little French—"

"—would make it Vietnamese," said Max.

"My, my, a critic. Dear Max, do make yourself useful, would you, and pour some wine? Where in heaven's name is Logan?" She turned to Inga. "You guys haven't frightened him off, I hope?"

"He was here a minute ago, asking about the lo mein."

"Well, where is he? Gone hiding?"

"In the study, I think," said Max. "Want me to fetch him?"

"No, I'll do it. You three relax. Start with the har-gow, they should be done."

As she left the room, Dan threw her a beseeching glance, as if to say, *don't go yet, I hardly know these people!* She smiled encouragingly, and tracked back through the living-room over to the study. The door was shut. She knocked. Nothing. She knocked again and opened the door a crack to find Logan hooked up to his iPod nano, and doing something on his laptop, wholly oblivious. She tapped him on the shoulder. He ripped the ear buds off.

"Sorry! Is the storm any worse?"

She frowned. "A little, but what I really came to say is that dinner's ready."

"Oh." He shut down the computer.

"*Oh?* That's it? Aren't you hungry?"

"Sure, yeah, it's not that—I mean, sure I'm hungry and all. I just feel, well, like soooo out of place, Dr. Holt—"

"Claire. And I know. But they're just people."

"Your people, your family—"

"Well, now, Daniel Starbuck has just arrived and I can see he's feeling just about as awkward as you are, so you two should join forces."

Logan brightened. "Mr. Arts and Science Celebration?"

"Yep, our Mr. AP. Did I tell you Josè has brought the University of Puerto Rico on board? And that I just volunteered to bring our traveling invertebrate lab to Gainesville? 'Kids and parents can to pick up gross marine animals,' that's what the director likes to say."

"Gross? I don't think they're gross."

Claire laughed. "Neither do I. But come now, before dinner gets cold or the storm does get worse."

With dogged reluctance, he stuffed his iPod nano in a pocket and trailed behind her back to the kitchen. Inga's hearty laughter greeted them.

"Oh, boy," she managed to say. "Don't get me started with the laughing."

Daniel smiled slyly. "Haven't you?"

She giggled. "Mom, you didn't tell me Mr. Starbuck did stand up comedy."

"I had no idea," said Claire. "Dan, you've met Logan?"

"Of course, up at the lab. Nice to see you again. Want a glass of wine?"

"There's beer, too," said Max.

Claire felt herself take a mental step away from being in the moment, to survey her kitchen, her burdened heart rising a little again, like a toy balloon, heliumed by small joy, and even if the stone of sadness held it back, the brief ascent was still there.

Look at my family, she mused. *A genetic stew, a mixed-up mixture of the globe, from Africa, to Denmark, from Japan to*

Ireland, hybrids, all of us. Poor Helga Crane. If only she could have been born at some later, less unforgiving moment. A piece of her grandmother's diary floated to mind…

…my sons and my daughter, they will grow to manhood, to womanhood in this vicious, hypocritical land. But at least they're black folk all together, not like me, hung as if from a noose between the two. I've been a fool, a damn fool, to let myself believe I could ever be happy! Fit in somewhere—least of all Denmark. To leave behind the city, and my books, my lovely, smart clothes for this loathsome quagmire of a life in Alabama—a life both better and far worse than the pale and powerful white world, which stole my birthright, my peace of mind, my life…

"Okay, then," Claire let out her breath with these words, breath that she hadn't realized she'd been holding. *Suicide*, she thought, *is not painless to those who live on without you.*

"People?" she said to her kitchen full of human and canine warmth, *as it should be*, she thought, *as it should always be, until it can no longer be—*

She smiled despite herself and clapped her hands. "Let's get this show on the road. Or on the table, at least."

A torrent pounded the roof, a piercing whistle, a sudden shuddering of the whole house woke her and she rolled over to the bare outline of Cooper at full attention next to her, tail tight, every muscle clenched for action. The house was pitch black, dead silent except for the raging weather outside.

"Power's gone off," she muttered. Already the air felt damply warm, too close.

Cooper growled, then woofed, quietly.

A heavy thump, roll, thump, something hit the roof and then the room was lit up, klieg-bright to an instant bang so guttural and deafening and visceral she flinched and cowered, thinking *we've been hit*. Cooper whined, shivering.

"Hey, baby, it's all right," she whispered, sitting up. Another flash-to-bang got her to her feet, fumbling for her robe, as Cooper nosed his head under the sheets. On bare feet, she crept carefully to her dresser; putting her palm firmly on top, she groped along until her fingertips found the flashlight she'd set there before going to bed. Gratefully, she switched it on, as another flash-to-bang shook the room. Rain pounded down; she could hear the gutter outside one corner of the bedroom overflow, unable to handle the flood.

Slowly she made her way down the hall, past the kitchen and study to the garage, Cooper at her heels; there, the downpour on the flat roof was murderously loud. She switched on the generator, and the house clicked back to life; the A/C kicked in, a few lights winked on but *the most vital thing*, she thought, *is Linkia* and with quick skipping steps she hurried out to the poolside aquarium, but Logan had beat her to it. His hair a tumble, in a pair of old gray sweats and shirt with a fading logo on the front, he looked almost child-like, peering into the tank. The glass of the porch shuddered and made a strange "foom" as the wind swept through, and the steady rains thrummed on.

"Everything okay?" she shouted over the fury.

"Looks like it," he shouted back. "Power wasn't out long enough to upset the tank's balance."

"Good. You okay?"

He glanced out across the pool at the absolute night. "I never knew rain could be like this. You can't see a thing out there. And the wind—"

Another flash whitened his already pale face but this time, it took a few moments before a long, drawn out drumbeat of the thunder's rumble followed.

"It's beginning to blow off already," she said. "Moving fast—still, dangerous."

"Mom?"

"Out here by the pool, Inga!"

"Dr. Holt?"

She turned back to Logan and smiled, whispering "Claire. Come on, you can say it. I know it's hard but—"

He blushed. "Claire. Is this a hurricane? This is what it's like?"

She frowned. "I think so. Sure feels like one."

Inga appeared at the threshold in her crimson robe, with Cooper panting beside her. "Claire is sleeping through this, can you believe it?" she said, raising her voice as she spoke. She stooped and picked up the dog. "But your baby, Mom, is one unhappy pup. I can feel him shivering."

"No, he doesn't like weather. Even a shower makes him glum. Come on, Logan, let's go back inside."

The three retreated from the noise of the porch, which muffled down to a mere bellow when Claire shut the French doors behind them. She took Cooper from Inga, saying, "First rainstorm we had after I brought him home, he hid under the bed until it stopped. Max asleep too?"

"No, when you got the generator going, he turned on the weather channel."

"So is it a real hurricane?" Logan cut in, with a suddenly roused eager curiosity.

"Fay's been upgraded, yeah," Inga replied. "If the weather channel is right, she's making landfall right here, right now—we are ground zero."

"Ground zero," said Claire, as she was hit by several grim flash memories—sheer drop into free fall, David's plane gone missing, swinging back to the dream she'd had in 'Frisco the night the dog Lulu had given her respite, broken test-tubes in the sand, her lab smashed to ruin which somehow lead to mind a snapshot of herself, sobbing into the flank of a golden dog, on a mountainside—she frowned, but the memory slipped, and collided with another flash-to-bang into which Max wandered, yawning. He looked around at the others and said, "Hurricane Fay."

"So it is, then," said Claire.

"Yup. For sure and tootin'."

"Why did you give up on the weather channel?" asked Inga.

"Because they're not telling us anything we can't feel for ourselves. Besides, I'm hungry, and we've got leftovers."

"You're *hungry?*" said Claire

Inga sighed. "He's always hungry."

Max shrugged and opened the refrigerator. "You don't mind, do you, Claire?"

"Of course not."

"Me too," said Logan sheepishly. "I mean a bite to eat sounds good."

"Well, while you two men chow down in the middle of a life-threatening hurricane, I'm going to check on my daughter," said Inga, striding for the hall.

"*Our* daughter," said Max, surveying the possibilities of a midnight snack, "is fearlessly sleeping through this threat to her life."

"Wisdom," said Claire, hugging Cooper close. "Back to beddie, my friend. Back to bed. Might as well try to sleep. Can't do a dang thing until Fay passes. If she passes—God, I wish you, Inga and baby Claire were safely up North."

"Don't be so gloomy, Claire. Fay isn't Katrina," said Max, but there was a tiny waver in his voice. He cleared his throat and took his voice down a notch into masculine reassurance. "Want something to eat?"

"Nah, you guys help yourselves."

Leaving Max and Logan to their excavation of the leftovers, Claire took Cooper to her room, where the muffled play of rain on roof was a little less ferocious then when it had wakened her. She set the terrier down on the bed, switched on a lamp, took the flashlight out of her pocket and put it back on the dresser; picked up her cell phone; no messages; snapped open her laptop, and onto email. No messages. Frustrated, she hopped onto the web, opened bookmarks, clicked Ruth's official Olympic blog where she found a newly uploaded shot of her daughter, smiling alongside text that read:

To all of you who've made this journey possible, my healed heart's thanks. When my Dad died, the old hole in my heart that a surgeon sewed up when I was a baby tore back open onto a void, and I couldn't figure out how to close it again. Being part of our American team, here in China, has put a patch on that sore place. If my Mom is reading this, Mom, I love you. I'm sure glad....

Tears made the rest blurry. Claire took a deep breath and turned away from the screen. *Finish it tomorrow*, she told herself, but tomorrow seemed far off, and just then she couldn't take more. Shuddering, she shut down the computer, snapped off the light, and crawled into bed. Lying on her side in the loudness and darkness of the storm, she let her stoicism desert her, lent herself to sobbing, her face against Cooper's warm flank until he shook her off, stepped onto her shoulder, and started licking the tears dry, which tickled and made her chuckle through the tightness in her throat.

"Stop that," she murmured. "Go on—"

Another flash turned the room grayish and for an instant, even less, Claire saw the darkness take on David's shape in the half-light, a lounging figure in that corner chair he'd so loved, his bony bare feet crossed on the ottoman, grinning with pure out-and-out lust, the lust that had always made her hair stand on end, a mutual lust out of which Ruth had come. She leaned into it, feeling the remembered weight of him, the flat, sparsely thatched expanse of his chest, the tall, spare richness of his male body, every inch she knew so well that every inch of her own skin ached with desire for contact, again.

When the room went dark, he went with it and she longed, suddenly and completely, to follow him. Now was the time.

"Wait for me—" she murmured, lying motionless, staring into nothing, as the rain yammered over her head. Cooper circled once and settled back to back with her, and at his touch, she felt her chest loosen, the stony weight rising off of it to meet the storm above, join it and bloom there like some odd black rose, bursting open, time-release, as if her anguish exulted in the sheer and immense, inhuman passion of weather.

Flash-bang.

She heard her father's voice launch itself at her out of the past, wheedling, "How will I just leave Claire, Jane? How? I can't do it—"

And her mother's voice, calm, resolute and ringing with a cold, self-righteous fury, "You won't have to. Claire and I will go—"

"And what about Honey?" said the memory.

"What about her? The dog stays. I can't afford to keep an animal."

"Then I'll have to give her away. Or put her down, Jane. You know I never wanted the damn dog. It belongs to Claire."

"Well, then? Put her down."

Honey!

She sat bolt upright. No wonder she'd run on those clumsy legs the little mermaid Star kept hidden, run up into the woods, half-blinded by tears, *we shall run away and hide together, Honey, forever and ever…*no. She shook her head. He didn't do that. He wouldn't do that. *It will pass,* she thought, staring into the ringing dark, and heard her mother's voice saying with a calm, cool certainty, *and this, too, my Dolly Dimples, this too shall pass* as she'd wept her teenaged heart out for what Jordan had done.

What happened to Honey?

She stared into the darkness. *I could ask Dad,* she thought, laying back down.

But no, Claire, don't, said Jane's voice. *Just let it go.*

And so she stared the past, and her ignorance of it, down, making it small, forcibly patching it over. *Nothing is forever and ever.*

She seldom prayed, but as the night drew on, long unused words of prayer came to her as comfort, *God grant me the serenity to accept the things I cannot change; courage to change the things I can; and the Wisdom to know the difference. Amen. What has been, has been, what will be…will be…or is it only Sinead O'Connor I'm hearing?* The words had come to her with that singer's Irish-Catholic lilt. She almost laughed at herself. *You can take the girl out of the church, but you can never take the church out of the girl.*

Despite the insane whine and intermittent howl of storm, then, she was able to doze a little, on and off until dawn, in short, swift dream sequences, slipping once, a mermaid again, into a bright, large pool of iridescent blue, as if the whole world had become *Linckia,* a blue so piercingly luminous it held her suspended in pure light. Bathed in this liquid rapture, the unadulterated color of purity, she felt a calm, a soothing so intense she wondered how she'd never noticed before that ecstasy existed. If only she could stay there, cradled in the beauty, forever…slowly, though, she rose from the mermaid's vision into a dank night sweat that made her push the comforter and sheets to her ankles. Awake then, the back of her neck and knees damp, she stared up at the full moon hanging in her bedroom skylight, glowing there like a cultured pearl in a platinum sky so clear, flat and polished it seemed the receding storm was steel-wool.

When she sat up, Cooper unfurled, all four paws in the air, for a belly rub. She stroked his pink flesh, then stood on the bed, balancing naked in the half-light, reaching childishly for the marble of moon, a reach that morphed into a stretch, then she stepped down, carefully, to the floor. Opening her dresser, she unfolded a lightweight sweat suit, found sneakers, socks. Dressed, she picked Cooper up and held him so tight in her arms, he yelped in fear.

"Sorry, boy," she whispered and, with him still in her arms, padded quietly down the sepia-lit hall. Pocketing keys she'd left on the kitchen island, Claire exited the house in the quieting storm, making straight away for the beach, and the ocean's bellow.

David, she thought, calm, clear-hearted. *I'm coming.*

The temperature had dropped from the close humid pre-hurricane night heat, into a mild, sultry-cool pre-dawn. As she walked down the road toward A1A with the dog cradled in her arms, the gentling air was stirred by a sea breeze. Jogging across the empty highway and onto a ramp, she clambered up the slight rise to the beach and set Cooper down in the sand. The blue-black sea chopped and heaved into rolling whitecaps that tore up to land. She knew that the riptides would be muscular, unforgiving, vicious. The dog bounced up and down around her legs as she pulled off her sneakers and socks. She tied the laces together and slung the sneakers over a shoulder, stuffing socks in a pocket, walking bare-foot as Cooper trotted merrily beside side. In a moment she stopped to bend down and roll up her cotton trousers so she could step into the roiling surf, still full of the impartial wrath called weather. The creamy breakers were high and blind-white, murmuring loudly out to a grumble, then thundering back in to land. Cooper began to saunter, sniffing along the grey expanse of the pounded flat beach, until he launched into sequence of figure eights that finally let him fly back to her, his tongue hanging out the side of his toothy smile.

"Hey, Coop," she said a she crouched, to gently grab his collar. "I think we've survived the storm." The dog tugged, eager. "Whoa, baby, calm down, calm down," she said and he put his front paws on her thigh. Then she released him, and the dog took like a shot, a terrier knot of speed, floppy ears flat, a racing ball of grey power.

Life itself, she thought, standing back and up squinting to watch as the dog grew smaller and smaller. *Ah, Buddy. Forgive me*. She turned to look over the waters again, as she stepped into the surf, wading out to her knees, staggering once or twice from the water's sinewy backhand.

I'm coming, she thought to him. *David—David*.

Another loud, smacking slap knocked her back, her feet slipped from under her, and as she tumbled forward, then back, arms flailing, in thrall to the living, grasping waters, as if in answer to that potency, the mermaid she had always been reared her spirit, rallied the animal strength of that mythical hybrid and propelled herself back to land with one sweeping blow, a starburst of resistance to the dark.

Gasping, rolling, she heard David's voice, clear, distinct, uncut by the swirl and boom of the sea. "Not now," the voice said. "Not now."

David!

She pulled herself to her elbows, spread-eagled and drenched, one knee throbbing, only to find herself staring into the seemingly worried brown eyes of Cooper, whining and growling, pawing at her hand. She got back up to a squat. "S'okay," she whispered to the dog. "S'okay, bud."

Unbidden, baby Claire's sleeping face came to view.

David.

She stood up, unsteady, thinking, *Ruth. Inga. They still need a Mom.*

Go home, whispered a voice, fading into the water's rumble.

"David?" but of course there was no answer and so she added, silently, *you will just have to wait for me.* Absently, she patted her pocket down, searching for keys. Her sneakers were gone. Crookedly, she smiled. *A keepsake for David?* she thought. *A mermaid doesn't need sneakers, does she?*

Gazing down the coast into the graying light, an eerie, skittering movement caught her eye. She picked up the dog, who seemed to grasp her neck with two paws, like a two-year old, holding on to her. "Look there, Coop," she whispered. All along the fringe where sand met scrub, a surreal, precise dance back and forth from burrow to water's edge and back of white to light yellow—

"—ghost crabs," she said and held him close, so that he wouldn't disrupt the kabuki theater of the feeding crabs. She stood, leaning her temple on the back of his head. The two of them stared at the rearing waters, still black and blue, under the flat iron of sky. A rare Luna moth flew valiantly against the wind, one large greenish wing tattered, all progress hindered by the steady breeze so that the insect hung, nearly motionless, at the skirt of the ocean.

He's beyond late in the season, thought Claire idly, watching until it came to her that so late in the season meant *he's dying.* She let her face grow wet again with windswept; Cooper, his coat curling in the sea tossed air, was damp against her chest, a chest which now felt and for the first time in a long time, light.

No, she thought, *I feel scoured.*

She could hear Cooper sniffing hard, sniff, sniff he caught a scent that made him bark. She looked up and saw the dark figure of a man, breasting against the wind toward her, listing to one side like a ship in distress.

Daniel.

"Look Coop," she murmured, "there's your boy. Go get him!" and she put the now squirming dog down so he could make a beeline to his boy. The phosphorescent green moth, suddenly gusted along by a shift in the sea-breeze, floated beside the running dog, as if in brief, silent communion— Claire watched the dying insect and the living dog bounce along in serendipity and thought, *that is so Disney and, well, kind of corny. Okay, very corny.* Yet it made her smile again as she thought, *but it's also just so damn ordinary. Thank God. An everyday, ordinary Florida morning, cooler than most, remarkably like spring.*

About the Author

After attending the Portland State University's Haystack Writing Workshop with Ursula K. Le Guin, Elizabeth Lynn and Vonda N. McIntyre, Stephanie A. Smith took her PhD in American Literature and Culture from UC Berkeley and is currently a full professor of English at the University of Florida where she teaches both literature and creative writing; prior to UF, she worked as a free-lance journalist, as an editor for *Western Imprints* in Portland, Oregon, as an assistant at *Glamour* and *Mademoiselle* magazines in New York City; at the academic journal *Representations* at Berkeley and at David Godine Publications in Boston, and is presently both a free-lance writing consultant, and an academic consultant for *Feminist Studies*. She is the author of the novels *The Warpaint Trilogy* (2012-14): *Warpaint, Baby Rocket,* and *Content Burns*; *Other Nature* (1995-7—long-listed for the Tiptree Award); *The-Boy-Who-Was-Thrown-Away* and *Snow-Eyes* (1985/87); academic criticism *Conceived By Liberty* (Cornell 1995—short-listed for the MLA First Book Award) and *Household Words* (Minnesota 2006); as well as numerous short stories, creative non-fiction and scholarly essays published in journals such as *New Letters,*

Asimov's, differences, genders, American Literature, and *Genre*. She has held fiction residencies at the Writer's Colony, the VCCA, the Noepe Center, Hedgebrook, Norcroft, Provincetown and Dorland and was an NEH Scholar at UCLA under the direction of N. Katherine Hayles; in 2015 she won a UF Rothman Summer Research Grant for fiction.